Folk Tales Every Child Should Know

Edited by
Hamilton Wright Mabie

FOLK TALES
Every Child Should Know

EDITED BY

Hamilton Wright Mabie

THE WHAT-EVERY-CHILD-
SHOULD-KNOW-LIBRARY

Published by
DOUBLEDAY, DORAN & CO., INC., *for*
THE PARENTS' INSTITUTE, INC.
Publishers of "The Parents' Magazine"
9 EAST 40th STREET, NEW YORK

FOLK TALES

Every Child Should Know

EDITED BY

Hamilton Wright Mabie

THE WHAT-EVERY-CHILD-SHOULD-KNOW-LIBRARY

ACKNOWLEDGMENTS

The editor and publishers wish to express their appreciation to the following firms for permission to use the material indicated:

To Messrs. G.P. Putnam's Sons for "Why the Sea is Salt, " "The Lad Who Went to the North Wind, " "The Lad and the Deil, " and "Ananzi and the Lion, " by Sir George Webbe Dasent, D.C. L.; to the Macmillan Company, New York, for "The Grateful Foxes" and "The Badger's Money, " by A. B. Mitford; to Messrs. Macmillan & Company, London, for "The Origin of Rubies, " by Rev. Lal Behari Day; to Messrs. Charles Scribner's Sons for "The Dun Horse, " by George Bird Grinnell; to Messrs. Little, Brown & Company for "The Peasant Story of Napoleon, " by Honoré de Balzac; to Messrs. Houghton, Mifflin & Company for "Why Brother Bear Has No Tail, " by Joel Chandler Harris, and for the following selections from "Sixty Folk Tales, from Exclusively Slavonic Sources, " translated by A. H. Wratislaw, M.A. : — "Long, Broad, and Sharpsight, " "Intelligence and Luck, " "George and the Goat, " "The Wonderful Hair, " "The Dragon and the Prince, " and "The Good Children. "

CONTENTS

INTRODUCTION

INTRODUCTION

When the traveller looks at Rome for the first time he does not realize that there have been several cities on the same piece of ground, and that the churches and palaces and other great buildings he sees to-day rest on an earlier and invisible city buried in dust beneath the foundations of the Rome of the Twentieth Century. In like manner, and because all visible things on the surface of the earth have grown out of older things which have ceased to be, the world of habits, the ideas, customs, fancies, and arts, in which we live is a survival of a younger world which long ago disappeared. When we speak of Friday as an unlucky day, or touch wood after saying that we have had good luck for a long time, or take the trouble to look at the new moon over the right shoulder, or avoid crossing the street while a funeral is passing, we are recalling old superstitions or beliefs, a vanished world in which our remote forefathers lived.

We do not realize how much of this vanished world still survives in our language, our talk, our books, our sculpture and pictures. The plays of Shakespeare are full of reference to the fancies and beliefs of the English people in his time or in the times not long before him. If we could understand all these references as we read, we should find ourselves in a world as different from the England of to-day as England is from Austria, and among a people whose ideas and language we should find it hard to understand.

In those early days there were no magazines or newspapers, and for the people as contrasted with the scholars there were no books. The most learned men were ignorant of things which intelligent children know to-day; only a very few men and women could read or write; and all kinds of beliefs about animals, birds, witches, fairies, giants, and the magical qualities of herbs and stones flourished like weeds in a neglected garden. There came into existence an immense mass of misinformation about all manner of things; some of it very stupid, much of it very poetic and interesting. Below the region of exact knowledge accessible to men of education, lay a region of popular fancies, ideas, proverbs, and superstitions in which the great mass of men and women lived, and which was a kind of invisible playground for children. Much of the popular belief about animals and the world was touched with imagination and was full of suggestions, illustrations, and pictorial figures which the poets were quick to use. When the king says to Cranmer in "Henry VIII: "

"Come, come, my lord, you'd spare your spoons, " he was thinking of the old custom of giving children at christenings silver or gilt spoons with handles shaped to represent the figures of the Apostles. Rich people gave twelve of the "apostles' spoons; " people of more moderate means gave three or four, or only one with the figure of the saint after whom the child was named. On Lord Mayor's Day in London, which came in November and is still celebrated, though shorn of much of its ancient splendour, the Lord Mayor's fool, as part of the festivities, jumped into a great bowl of custard, and this is what Ben Jonson had in mind when he wrote:

> "He may, perchance, in tail of a sheriff's dinner,
> Skip with a rime o' the table, from near nothing,
> And take his almain leap into a custard,
> Shall make my lady Maydress and her sisters,
> Laugh all their hoods over their shoulders. "

It was once widely believed that a stone of magical, medicinal qualities was set in the toad's head, and so Shakespeare wrote:

> "Sweet are the uses of adversity;
> Which, like the toad, ugly and venomous,
> Wears yet a precious jewel in its head. "

"A Midsummer Night's Dream" is the most wonderful fairy story in the world, but Shakespeare did not create it out of hand; he found the fairy part of it in the traditions of the country people. One of his most intelligent students says: "He founded his elfin world on the prettiest of the people's traditions, and has clothed it in the ever-living flower of his own exuberant fancy. "

This immense mass of belief, superstition, fancy, is called folk-lore and is to be found in all parts of the world. These fancies or faiths or superstitions were often distorted with stories, and side by side with folk-lore grew up the folk-tales, of which there are so many that a man might spend his whole life writing them down. They were not made as modern stories are often made, by men who think out carefully what they are to say, arrange the different parts so that they go together like the parts of a house or of a machine, and write them with careful selection of words so as to make the story vivid and interesting.

The folk-tales were not written out; many of them grew out of single incidents or little inventions of fancy, and became longer and larger as they passed from one story-teller to another and were retold generation after generation.

Men love stories, and for very good reasons, as has been pointed out in introductions to other volumes in this series; and the more quick and original the imagination of a race, the more interesting and varied will be its stories. From the earliest times, long before books were made, the people of many countries were eagerly listening to the men and women who could tell thrilling or humorous tales, as in these later days they read the novels of the writers who know how to tell a story so as to stir the imagination or hold the attention and make readers forget themselves and their worries and troubles. In India and Japan, in Russia and Roumania, among the Indians at the foot of the Rocky Mountains, these stories are still told, not only to children by their mothers and grandmothers, but to crowds of grown-up people by those who have the art of making tales entertaining; and there are still so many of these stories floating about the world from one person to another that if they were written down they would fill a great library. "Until the generation now lately passed away, " says Mr. Gosse in his introduction to that very interesting book, "Folk and Fairy Tales" by Asbjörnsen, "almost the only mode in which the Norwegian peasant killed time in the leisure moments between his daily labour and his religious observances, was in listening to stories. It was the business of old men and women who had reached the extreme limit of their working hours, to retain and repeat these ancient legends in prose and verse, and to recite or sing them when called to do so. " And Miss Hapgood has told us that in Russia these stories have not only been handed down wholly by word or mouth for a thousand years, but are flourishing to-day and extending into fresh fields.

The stories made by the people, and told before evening fires, or in public places and at the gates of inns in the Orient, belong to the ages when books were few and knowledge limited, or to people whose fancy was not hampered by familiarity with or care for facts; they are the creations, as they were the amusement, of men and women who were children in knowledge, but were thinking deeply and often wisely of what life meant to them, and were eager to know and hear more about themselves, their fellows, and the world. In the earlier folk-stories one finds a childlike simplicity and readiness to believe in the marvellous; and these qualities are found also in the French peasant's version of the career of Napoleon.

HAMILTON W. MABIE

I

HANS IN LUCK

Hans had served his Master seven years, and at the end of that time he said to him: "Master, since my time is up, I should like to go home to my mother; so give me my wages, if you please. "

His Master replied, "You have served me truly and honestly, Hans, and such as your service was, such shall be your reward; " and with these words he gave him a lump of gold as big as his head. Hans thereupon took his handkerchief out of his pocket, and, wrapping the gold up in it, threw it over his shoulder and set out on the road toward his native village. As he went along, carefully setting one foot to the ground before the other, a horseman came in sight, trotting gaily and briskly along upon a capital animal. "Ah, " said Hans, aloud, "what a fine thing that riding is! one is seated, as it were, upon a stool, kicks against no stones, spares one's shoes, and gets along without any trouble! "

The Rider, overhearing Hans making these reflections, stopped and said, "Why, then, do you travel on foot, my fine fellow? "

"Because I am forced, " replied Hans, "for I have got a bit of a lump to carry home; it certainly is gold, but then I can't carry my head straight, and it hurts my shoulder. "

"If you like we will exchange, " said the Rider. "I will give you my horse, and you can give me your lump of gold. "

"With all my heart, " cried Hans; "but I tell you fairly you undertake a very heavy burden. "

The man dismounted, took the gold, and helped Hans on to the horse, and, giving him the reins into his hands, said, "Now, when you want to go faster, you must chuckle with your tongue and cry, 'Gee up! gee up! '"

Hans was delighted indeed when he found himself on the top of a horse, and riding along so freely and gaily. After a while he thought he should like to go rather quicker, and so he cried, "Gee up! gee up! " as the man had told him. The horse soon set off at a hard trot, and, before Hans knew what he was about, he was thrown over head and heels into a ditch which divided the fields from the road. The horse, having accomplished this feat, would have bolted off if he had not been stopped by a Peasant who was coming that way, driving a cow before him. Hans soon picked himself up on his legs, but he was terribly put out, and said to the countryman, "That is bad sport, that riding, especially when one mounts such a beast as that, which stumbles and throws one off so as to nearly break one's neck. I will never ride on that animal again. Commend me to your cow: one may walk behind her without any discomfort, and besides one has, every day for certain, milk, butter, and cheese. Ah! what would I not give for such a cow! "

"Well, " said the Peasant, "such an advantage you may soon enjoy; I will exchange my cow for your horse. "

To this Hans consented with a thousand thanks, and the Peasant, swinging himself upon the horse, rode off in a hurry.

Hans now drove his cow off steadily before him, thinking of his lucky bargain in this wise: "I have a bit of bread, and I can, as often as I please, eat with it butter and cheese, and when I am thirsty I can milk my cow and have a draught: and what more can I desire? "

As soon, then, as he came to an inn he halted, and ate with great satisfaction all the bread he had brought with him for his noonday and evening meals, and washed it down with a glass of beer, to buy which he spent his two last farthings. This over, he drove his cow farther, but still in the direction of his mother's village. The heat meantime became more and more oppressive as noontime approached, and just then Hans came to a common which was an hour's journey across. Here he got into such a state of heat that his tongue clave to the roof of his mouth, and he thought to himself: "This won't do; I will just milk my cow, and refresh myself. " Hans, therefore tied her to a stump of a tree, and, having no pail, placed his leathern cap below, and set to work, but not a drop of milk could he squeeze out. He had placed himself, too, very awkwardly, and at last the impatient cow gave him such a kick on the head that he tumbled over on the ground, and for a long time knew not where he was. Fortunately, not many hours after, a Butcher passed by, trundling a young pig along upon a wheelbarrow. "What trick is this! " exclaimed he, helping up poor Hans; and Hans told him that all that had passed. The Butcher then handed him his flask and said, "There, take a drink; it will revive you. Your cow might well give no milk: she is an old beast, and worth nothing at the best but for the plough or the butcher! "

"Eh! eh! " said Hans, pulling his hair over his eyes, "who would have thought it? It is all very well when one can kill a beast like that at home, and make a profit of the flesh; but for my part I have no relish for cow's flesh; it is too tough for me! Ah! a young pig like yours is the thing that tastes something like, let alone the sausages! "

"Well now, for love of you, " said the Butcher, "I will make an exchange, and let you have my pig for your cow. "

"Heaven reward you for your kindness! " cried Hans; and, giving up the cow, he untied the pig from the barrow and took into his hands the string with which it was tied.

Hans walked on again, considering how everything had happened just as he wished, and how all his vexations had turned out for the best after all! Presently a boy overtook him carrying a fine white goose under his arm, and after they had said "Good-day" to each other, Hans began to talk about his luck, and what profitable exchanges he had made. The Boy on his part told him that he was carrying the goose to a christening-feast. "Just lift it, " said he to Hans, holding it up by its wings, "just feel how heavy it is; why, it has been fattened up for the last eight weeks, and whoever bites it when it is cooked will have to wipe the grease from each side of his mouth! "

"Yes, " said Hans, weighing it with one hand, "it is weighty, but my pig is no trifle either. "

While he was speaking the Boy kept looking about on all sides, and shaking his head suspiciously, and at length he broke out, "I am afraid it is not all right about your pig. In the village through which I have just come, one has been stolen out of the sty of the mayor himself; and I am afraid, very much afraid, you have it now in your hand! They have sent out several people, and it would be a very bad job for you if they found you with the pig; the best thing you can do is to hide it in some dark corner! "

Honest Hans was thunderstruck, and exclaimed, "Ah, Heaven help me in this fresh trouble! you know the neighbourhood better than I do; do you take my pig and let me have your goose, " said he to the boy.

"I shall have to hazard something at that game, " replied the Boy, "but still I do not wish to be the cause of your meeting with misfortune; " and, so saying, he took the rope into his own hand, and drove the pig off quickly by a side-path, while Hans, lightened of his cares, walked on homeward with the goose under his arm. "If I judge rightly, " thought he to himself, "I have gained even by this exchange: first there is a good roast; then the quantity of fat which will drip out will make goose broth for a quarter of a year; and then there are fine white feathers, which, when once I have put into my pillow I warrant I shall sleep without rocking. What pleasure my mother will have! "

As he came to the last village on his road there stood a Knife-grinder, with his barrow by the hedge, whirling his wheel round and singing:

> "Scissors and razors and such-like I grind;
> And gaily my rags are flying behind. "

Hans stopped and looked at him, and at last he said, "You appear to have a good business, if I may judge by your merry song? "

"Yes, " answered the Grinder, "this business has a golden bottom! A true knife-grinder is a man who as often as he puts his hand into his pocket feels money in it! But what a fine goose you have got; where did you buy it? "

"I did not buy it at all, " said Hans, "but took it in exchange for my pig. " "And the pig? " "I exchanged for my cow. " "And the cow? " "I exchanged a horse for her. " "And the horse? " "For him I gave a lump of gold as big as my head. " "And the gold? " "That was my wages for a seven years' servitude. " "And I see you have known how to benefit yourself each time, " said the Grinder; "but, could you now manage that you heard the money rattling in your pocket as you walked, your fortune would be made. "

"Well! how shall I manage that? " asked Hans.

"You must become a grinder like me; to this trade nothing peculiar belongs but a grindstone; the other necessaries find themselves. Here

4

is one which is a little worn, certainly, and so I will not ask anything more for it than your goose; are you agreeable? ”

“How can you ask me? ” said Hans; “why, I shall be the luckiest man in the world; having money as often as I dip my hand into my pocket, what have I to care about any longer? ”

So saying, he handed over the goose, and received the grindstone in exchange.

“Now, ” said the Grinder, picking up an ordinary big flint stone which lay near, “now, there you have a capital stone upon which only beat them long enough and you may straighten all your old nails! Take it, and use it carefully! ”

Hans took the stone and walked on with a satisfied heart, his eyes glistening with joy. “I must have been born, ” said he, “to a heap of luck; everything happens just as I wish, as if I were a Sunday-child. ”

Soon, however, having been on his legs since daybreak, he began to feel very tired, and was plagued too with hunger, since he had eaten all his provision at once in his joy about the cow bargain. At last he felt quite unable to go farther, and was forced, too, to halt every minute for the stones encumbered him very much. Just then the thought overcame him, what a good thing it were if he had no need to carry them any longer, and at the same moment he came up to a stream. Here he resolved to rest and refresh himself with drink, and so that the stones might not hurt him in kneeling he laid them carefully down by his side on the bank. This done, he stooped down to scoop up some water in his hand, and then it happened that he pushed one stone a little too far, so that both presently went plump into the water. Hans, as soon as he saw them sinking to the bottom, jumped up for joy, and then kneeled down and returned thanks, with tears in his eyes, that so mercifully, and without any act on his part, and in so nice a way, he had been delivered from the heavy stones, which alone hindered him from getting on.

“So lucky as I am, ” exclaimed Hans, “is no other man under the sun! ”

Then with a light heart, and free from every burden, he leaped gaily along till he reached his mother’s house.

II

WHY THE SEA IS SALT

Once on a time, but it was a long, long time ago, there were two brothers, one rich and one poor. Now, one Christmas eve, the poor one hadn't so much as a crumb in the house, either of meat or bread, so he went to his brother to ask him for something to keep Christmas with, in God's name. It was not the first time his brother had been forced to help him, and you may fancy he wasn't very glad to see his face, but he said:

"If you will do what I ask you to do, I'll give you a whole flitch of bacon. "

So the poor brother said he would do anything and was full of thanks.

"Well, here is the flitch, " said the rich brother, "and now go straight to Hell. "

"What I have given my word to do, I must stick to, " said the other; so he took the flitch and set off. He walked the whole day, and at dusk he came to a place where he saw a very bright light.

"Maybe this is the place, " said the man to himself. So he turned aside, and the first thing he saw was an old, old man, with a long white beard, who stood in an outhouse, hewing wood for the Christmas fire.

"Good even, " said the man with the flitch.

"The same to you; whither are you going so late? " said the man.

"Oh! I'm going to Hell, if I only knew the right way, " answered the poor man.

"Well, you're not far wrong, for this is Hell, " said the old man; "when you get inside they will be all for buying your flitch, for meat is scarce in Hell; but, mind you don't sell it unless you get the hand-quern which stands behind the door for it. When you come out, I'll

6

teach you how to handle the quern, for it's good to grind almost anything. "

So the man with the flitch thanked the other for his good advice, and gave a great knock at the Devil's door.

When he got in, everything was just as the old man had said. All the devils, great and small, came swarming up to him like ants round an anthill, and each tried to outbid the other for the flitch.

"Well! " said the man, "by rights, my old dame and I ought to have this flitch for our Christmas dinner; but since you have all set your hearts on it, I suppose I must give it up to you; but if I sell it at all, I'll have for it the quern behind the door yonder. "

At first the Devil wouldn't hear of such a bargain, and chaffed and haggled with the man; but he stuck to what he said, and at last the Devil had to part with his quern. When the man got out into the yard, he asked the old woodcutter how he was to handle the quern; and after he had learned how to use it, he thanked the old man and went off home as fast as he could, but still the clock had struck twelve on Christmas eve before he reached his own door.

"Wherever in the world have you been? " said his old dame; "here have I sat hour after hour waiting and watching, without so much as two sticks to lay together under the Christmas brose. "

"Oh! " said the man, "I couldn't get back before, for I had to go a long way first for one thing, and then for another; but now you shall see what you shall see. "

So he put the quern on the table, and bade it first of all grind lights, then a table-cloth, then meat, then ale, and so on till they had got everything that was nice for Christmas fare. He had only to speak the word, and the quern ground out what he wanted. The old dame stood by blessing her stars, and kept on asking where he had got this wonderful quern, but he wouldn't tell her.

"It's all one where I got it from; you see the quern is a good one, and the mill-stream never freezes, that's enough. "

So he ground meat and drink and dainties enough to last out till Twelfth Day, and on the third day he asked all his friends and kin to his house, and gave a great feast. Now, when his rich brother saw all that was on the table, and all that was behind in the larder, he grew quite spiteful and wild, for he couldn't bear that his brother should have anything.

"Twas only on Christmas eve, " he said to the rest, "he was in such straits that he came and asked for a morsel of food in God's name, and now he gives a feast as if he were count or king; " and he turned to his brother and said:

"But whence, in Hell's name, have you got all this wealth? "

"From behind the door, " answered the owner of the quern, for he didn't care to let the cat out of the bag. But later on in the evening, when he had got a drop too much, he could keep his secret no longer, and brought out the quern and said:

"There, you see what has gotten me all this wealth; " and so he made the quern grind all kind of things. When his brother saw it, he set his heart on having the quern, and, after a deal of coaxing, he got it; but he had to pay three hundred dollars for it, and his brother bargained to keep it till hay-harvest, for he thought, if I keep it till then, I can make it grind meat and drink that will last for years. So you may fancy the quern didn't grow rusty for want of work, and when hay-harvest came, the rich brother got it, but the other took care not to teach him how to handle it.

It was evening when the rich brother got the quern home, and the next morning he told his wife to go out into the hay-field and toss, while the mowers cut the grass, and he would stay at home and get the dinner ready. So, when dinner-time drew near, he put the quern on the kitchen table and said:

"Grind herrings and broth, and grind them good and fast. "

So the quern began to grind herrings and broth; first of all, all the dishes full, then all the tubs full, and so on till the kitchen floor was quite covered. Then the man twisted and twirled at the quern to get it to stop, but for all his twisting and fingering the quern went on grinding, and in a little while the broth rose so high that the man was like to drown. So he threw open the kitchen door and ran into the parlour, but it wasn't long before the quern had ground the parlour full too, and it was only at the risk of his life that the man could get hold of the latch of the house door through the stream of broth. When he got the door open, he ran out and set off down the road, with the stream of herrings and broth at his heels, roaring like a waterfall over the whole farm.

Now, his old dame, who was in the field tossing hay, thought it a long time to dinner, and at last she said:

"Well! though the master doesn't call us home, we may as well go. Maybe he finds it hard work to boil the broth, and will be glad of my help. "

The men were willing enough, so they sauntered homeward; but just as they had got a little way up the hill, what should they meet but herrings, and broth, and bread, all running and dashing, and splashing together in a stream, and the master himself running before them for his life, and as he passed them he bawled out: "Would to heaven each of you had a hundred throats! but take care you're not drowned in the broth. "

Away he went, as though the Evil One were at his heels, to his brother's house, and begged him for God's sake to take back the quern that instant; for, said he:

"If it grinds only one hour more, the whole parish will be swallowed up by herrings and broth. "

But his brother wouldn't hear of taking it back till the other paid him down three hundred dollars more.

So the poor brother got both the money and the quern, and it wasn't long before he set up a farmhouse far finer than the one in which his brother lived, and with the quern he ground so much gold that he covered it with plates of gold; and as the farm lay by the sea-side, the golden house gleamed and glistened far away over the sea. All who sailed by, put ashore to see the rich man in the golden house, and to see the wonderful quern, the fame of which spread far and wide, till there was nobody who hadn't heard tell of it.

So one day there came a skipper who wanted to see the quern; and the first thing he asked was if it could grind salt.

"Grind salt! " said the owner; "I should just think it could. It can grind anything. "

When the skipper heard that, he said he must have the quern, cost what it would; for if he only had it, he thought he should be rid of his long voyages across stormy seas for a lading of salt. Well, at first the man wouldn't hear of parting with the quern; but the skipper begged and prayed so hard that at last he let him have it, but he had to pay many, many thousand dollars for it. Now, when the skipper had got the quern on his back, he soon made off with it, for he was afraid lest the man should change his mind; so he had no time to ask how to handle the quern, but got on board his ship as fast as he could, and set sail. When he had sailed a good way off, he brought the quern on deck and said:

"Grind salt, and grind both good and fast. "

Well, the quern began to grind salt so that it poured out like water; and when the skipper had got the ship full, he wished to stop the quern, but whichever way he turned it, and however much he tried, it was no good; the quern kept grinding on, and the heap of salt grew higher and higher, and at last down sunk the ship.

There lies the quern at the bottom of the sea, and grinds away at this very day, and that's why the sea is salt.

III

THE LAD WHO WENT TO THE NORTH WIND

Once on a time there was an old widow who had one son and, as she was poorly and weak, her son had to go up into the safe to fetch meal for cooking; but when he got outside the safe, and was just going down the steps, there came the North Wind, puffing and blowing, caught up the meal, and so away with it through the air. Then the lad went back into the safe for more; but when he came out again on the steps, if the North Wind didn't come again and carry off the meal with a puff; and more than that, he did so the third time. At this the lad got very angry; and as he thought it hard that the North Wind should behave so, he thought he'd just look him up, and ask him to give up his meal.

So off he went, but the way was long, and he walked and walked; but at last he came to the North Wind's house.

"Good day! " said the lad, and "thank you for coming to see us yesterday. "

"GOOD DAY! " answered the North Wind, for his voice was loud and gruff, "AND THANKS FOR COMING TO SEE ME. WHAT DO YOU WANT? "

"Oh! " answered the lad, "I only wished to ask you to be so good as to let me have back that meal you took from me on the safe steps, for we haven't much to live on; and if you're to go on snapping up the morsel we have there'll be nothing for it but to starve. "

"I haven't got your meal, " said the North Wind; "but if you are in such need, I'll give you a cloth which will get you everything you want, if you only say, 'Cloth, spread yourself, and serve up all kinds of good dishes! '"

With this the lad was well content. But, as the way was so long he couldn't get home in one day, he turned into an inn on the way; and when they were going to sit down to supper, he laid the cloth on a table which stood in the corner and said:

"Cloth spread yourself, and serve up all kinds of good dishes. "

He had scarce said so before the cloth did as it was bid; and all who stood by thought it a fine thing, but most of all the landlady. So, when all were fast asleep, at dead of night, she took the lad's cloth, and put another in its stead, just like the one he had got from the North Wind, but which couldn't so much as serve up a bit of dry bread.

So, when the lad woke, he took his cloth and went off with it, and that day he got home to his mother.

"Now, " said he, "I've been to the North Wind's house, and a good fellow he is, for he gave me this cloth, and when I only say to it, 'Cloth, spread yourself, and serve up all kinds of good dishes, ' I get any sort of food I please. "

"All very true, I dare say, " said his mother; "but seeing is believing, and I shan't believe it till I see it. "

So the lad made haste, drew out a table, laid the cloth on it, and said:

"Cloth, spread yourself, and serve all up kinds of good dishes. "

But never a bit of dry bread did the cloth serve up.

"Well, " said the lad, "there's no help for it but to go to the North Wind again; " and away he went.

So he came to where the North Wind lived late in the afternoon.

"Good evening! " said the lad.

"Good evening, " said the North Wind.

"I want my rights for that meal of ours which you took, " said the lad; "for as for that cloth I got, it isn't worth a penny. "

"I've got no meal, " said the North Wind; "but yonder you have a ram which coins nothing but golden ducats as soon as you say to it:

"'Ram, ram! make money! '"

So the lad thought this a fine thing but as it was too far to get home that day, he turned in for the night to the same inn where he had slept before.

Before he called for anything, he tried the truth of what the North Wind had said of the ram, and found it all right; but when the landlord saw that, he thought it was a famous ram, and, when the lad had fallen asleep, he took another which couldn't coin gold ducats, and changed the two.

Next morning off went the lad; and when he got home to his mother he said:

"After all, the North Wind is a jolly fellow; for now he has given me a ram which can coin golden ducats if I only say, 'Ram, ram! make money!'"

"All very true, I dare say, " said his mother; "but I shan't believe any such stuff until I see the ducats made. "

"Ram, ram! make money! " said the lad; but if the ram made anything it wasn't money.

So the lad went back again to the North Wind and blew him up, and said the ram was worth nothing, and he must have his rights for the meal.

"Well, " said the North Wind; "I've nothing else to give you but that old stick in the corner yonder; but it's a stick of that kind that if you say:

"'Stick, stick! lay on! ' it lays on till you say:

"'Stick, stick! now stop! '"

So, as the way was long, the lad turned in this night too to the landlord; but as he could pretty well guess how things stood as to the cloth and the ram, he lay down at once on the bench and began to snore, as if he were asleep.

Now the landlord, who easily saw that the stick must be worth something, hunted up one which was like it, and when he heard the lad snore, was going to change the two, but just as the landlord was about to take it the lad bawled out:

"Stick, stick! lay on! "

So the stick began to beat the landlord, till he jumped over chairs, and tables, and benches, and yelled and roared:

"Oh my! oh my! bid the stick be still, else it will beat me to death, and you shall have back both your cloth and your ram. "

When the lad thought the landlord had got enough, he said:

"Stick, stick! now stop! "

Then he took the cloth and put it into his pocket, and went home with his stick in his hand, leading the ram by a cord round its horns; and so he got his rights for the meal he had lost.

IV

THE LAD AND THE DEIL

Once on a time there was a lad who was walking along a road cracking nuts, so he found one that was worm-eaten, and just at that very moment he met the Deil.

"Is it true, now, " said the lad, "what they say, that the Deil can make himself as small as he chooses, and thrust himself on through a pinhole? "

"Yes, it is, " said the Deil.

"Oh! it is, is it? then let me see you do it, and just creep into this nut, " said the lad.

So the Deil did it.

Now, when he had crept well into it through the worm's hole, the lad stopped it up with a pin.

"Now, I've got you safe, " he said, and put the nut into his pocket.

So when he had walked on a bit, he came to a smithy, and he turned in and asked the smith if he'd be good enough to crack that nut for him.

"Ay, that'll be an easy job, " said the smith, and took his smallest hammer, laid the nut on the anvil, and gave it a blow, but it wouldn't break.

So he took another hammer a little bigger, but that wasn't heavy enough either.

Then he took one bigger still, but it was still the same story; and so the smith got wroth, and grasped his great sledge-hammer.

"Now, I'll crack you to bits, " he said, and let drive at the nut with all his might and main. And so the nut flew to pieces with a bang that blew off half the roof of the smithy, and the whole house creaked and groaned as though it were ready to fall.

15

"Why! if I don't think the Deil must have been in that nut, " said the smith.

"So he was; you're quite right, " said the lad, as he went away laughing.

V

ANANZI AND THE LION

Once on a time Ananzi planned a scheme. He went to town and bought ever so many firkins of fat, and ever so many sacks, and ever so many balls of string, and a very big frying pan, then he went to the bay and blew a shell, and called the Head-fish in the sea, "Green Eel, " to him. Then he said to the fish, "The King sends me to tell you that you must bring all the fish on shore, for he wants to give them new life. "

So "Green Eel" said he would, and went to call them. Meanwhile Ananzi lighted a fire, and took out some of the fat, and got his frying pan ready, and as fast as the fish came out of the water he caught them and put them into the frying pan, and so he did with all of them until he got to the Head-fish, who was so slippery that he couldn't hold him, and he got back again into the water.

When Ananzi had fried all the fish, he put them into the sacks, and took the sacks on his back, and set off to the mountains. He had not gone very far when he met Lion, and Lion said to him:

"Well, brother Ananzi, where have you been? I have not seen you a long time. "

Ananzi said, "I have been travelling about. "

"Oh! But what have you got there? " said the Lion.

"Oh! I have got my mother's bones—she has been dead these forty-eleven years, and they say I must not keep her here, so I am taking her up into the middle of the mountains to bury her. "

Then they parted. After he had gone a little way, the Lion said: "I know that Ananzi is a great rogue; I dare say he has got something there that he doesn't want me to see, and I will just follow him; " but he took care not to let Ananzi see him.

Now, when Ananzi got into the wood, he set his sacks down, and took one fish out and began to eat; then a fly came, and Ananzi said, "I cannot eat any more, for there is some one near; " so he tied the sack up, and went on farther into the mountains, where he set his sacks down, and took out two fish which he ate; and no fly came. He said, "There is no one near; " so he took out more fish. But when he had eaten about half a dozen the Lion came up and said:

"Well, brother Ananzi, a pretty tale you have told me. "

"Oh! brother Lion, I am so glad you have come; never mind what tale I have told you, but come and sit down—it was only my fun. "

So Lion sat down and began to eat; but before Ananzi had eaten two fish, Lion had emptied one of the sacks. Then said Ananzi to himself:

"Greedy fellow, eating up all my fish. "

"What do you say, sir? "

"I only said you do not eat half fast enough, " for he was afraid the Lion would eat him up.

Then they went on eating, but Ananzi wanted to revenge himself, and he said to the Lion, "Which of us do you think is the stronger? "

The Lion said, "Why, I am, of course. "

Then Ananzi said, "We will tie one another to the tree, and we shall see which is the stronger. "

Now they agreed that the Lion should tie Ananzi first, and he tied him with some very fine string, and did not tie him tight. Ananzi twisted himself about two or three times, and the string broke.

Then it was Ananzi's turn to tie the Lion, and he took some very strong cord. The Lion said, "You must not tie me tight, for I did not tie you tight. " And Ananzi said, "Oh! no, to be sure, I will not. " But he tied him as tight as ever he could, and then told him to try and get loose.

The Lion tried and tried in vain—he could not get loose. Then Ananzi thought, now is my chance; so he got a big stick and beat him, and then went away and left him, for he was afraid to loose him lest he should kill him.

Now there was a woman called Miss Nancy, who was going out one morning to get some "callalou" (spinach) in the wood, and as she was going she heard some one say, "Good morning, Miss Nancy! " She could not tell who spoke to her, but she looked where the voice came from, and saw the Lion tied to the tree.

"Good morning, Mr. Lion, what are you doing there? "

He said, "It is all that fellow Ananzi who has tied me to the tree, but will you loose me? "

But she said, "No, for I am afraid, if I do, you will kill me. " But he gave her his word he would not; still she could not trust him; but he begged her again and again, and said:

"Well, if I do try to eat you, I hope all the trees will cry out shame upon me. "

So at last she consented; but she had no sooner loosed him, than he came up to her to eat her, for he had been so many days without food that he was quite ravenous, but the trees immediately cried out, "Shame, " and so he could not eat her. Then she went away as fast as she could, and the Lion found his way home.

When Lion got home he told his wife and children all that happened to him, and how Miss Nancy had saved his life, so they said they would have a great dinner, and ask Miss Nancy. Now when Ananzi heard of it, he wanted to go to the dinner, so he went to Miss Nancy, and said she must take him with her as her child, but she said, "No. " Then he said, "I can turn myself into quite a little child and then you can take me, " and at last she said, "Yes; " and he told her, when she was asked what pap her baby ate, she must be sure to tell them it did not eat pap, but the same food as every one else; and so they went, and had a very good dinner, and set off home again—but somehow one of the Lion's sons fancied that all was not right, and he told his father he was sure it was Ananzi, and the Lion set out after him.

Now as they were going along, before the Lion got up to them, Ananzi begged Miss Nancy to put him down, that he might run, which he did, and he got away and ran along the wood, and the Lion ran after him. When he found the Lion was overtaking him, he turned himself into an old man with a bundle of wood on his head—

and when the Lion got up to him, he said, "Good morning, Mr. Lion, " and the Lion said, "Good morning, old gentleman. "

Then the old man said, "What are you after now? " and the Lion asked if he had seen Ananzi pass that way, but the old man said, "No, that fellow Ananzi is always meddling with some one; what mischief has he been up to now? "

Then the Lion told him, but the old man said it was no use to follow him any more, for he would never catch him, and so the Lion wished him good-day, and turned and went home again.

VI

THE GRATEFUL FOXES

One fine spring day two friends went out to a moor to gather fern, attended by a boy with a bottle of wine and a box of provisions. As they were straying about, they saw at the foot of a hill two foxes that had brought out their cub to play; and whilst they looked on, struck by the strangeness of the sight, three children came up from a neighbouring village with baskets in their hands, on the same errand as themselves. As soon as the children saw the foxes, they picked up a bamboo stick and took the creatures stealthily in the rear; and when the old foxes took to flight, they surrounded them and beat them with the stick, so that they ran away as fast as their legs could carry them; but two of the boys held down the cub, and, seizing it by the scruff of the neck, went off in high glee.

The two friends were looking on all the while, and one of them, raising his voice, shouted out, "Hallo! you boys! what are you doing with that fox? "

The eldest of the boys replied, "We're going to take him home and sell him to a young man in our village. He'll buy him, and then he'll boil him in a pot and eat him. "

"Well, " replied the other, after considering the matter attentively, "I suppose it's all the same to you whom you sell him to. You'd better let me have him. "

"Oh, but the young man from our village promised us a good sum if we could find a fox, and got us to come out to the hills and catch one; and so we can't sell him to you at any price. "

"Well, I suppose it cannot be helped, then; but how much would the young man give you for the cub? "

"Oh, he'll give us three hundred cash at least. "

"Then I'll give you half a bu; [1] and so you'll gain five hundred cash by the transaction. "

"Oh, we'll sell him for that, sir. How shall we hand him over to you? "

"Just tie him up here, " said the other; and so he made fast the cub round the neck with the string of the napkin in which the luncheon-box was wrapped, and gave half a bu to the three boys, who ran away delighted.

The man's friend, upon this, said to him: "Well, certainly you have got queer tastes. What on earth are you going to keep the fox for? "

"How very unkind of you to speak of my tastes like that. If we had not interfered just now, the fox's cub would have lost its life. If we had not seen the affair, there would have been no help for it. How could I stand by and see life taken? It was but a little I spent—only half a bu—to save the cub, but had it cost a fortune I should not have grudged it. I thought you were intimate enough with me to know my heart; but to-day you have accused me of being eccentric, and I see how mistaken I have been in you. However, our friendship shall cease from this day forth. "

And when he had said this with a great deal of firmness, the other, retiring backward and bowing with his hands on his knees, replied:

"Indeed, indeed, I am filled with admiration at the goodness of your heart. When I hear you speak thus, I feel more than ever how great is the love I bear you. I thought that you might wish to use the cub as a sort of decoy to lead the old ones to you, that you might pray them to bring prosperity and virtue to your house. When I called you eccentric just now, I was but trying your heart, because I had some suspicions of you; and now I am truly ashamed of myself. "

And as he spoke, still bowing, the other replied: "Really! was that indeed your thought? Then I pray you to forgive me for my violent language. "

When the two friends had thus become reconciled, they examined the cub, and saw that it had a slight wound in its foot, and could not walk; and while they were thinking what they should do, they spied out the herb called "Doctor's Nakasé, " which was just sprouting; so they rolled up a little of it in their fingers and applied it to the part. Then they pulled out some boiled rice from their luncheon-box and offered it to the cub, but it showed no sign of wanting to eat; so they stroked it gently on the back and petted it; and as the pain of the wound seemed to have subsided, they were admiring the properties of the herb, when, opposite to them, they saw the old foxes sitting watching them by the side of some stacks of rice straw.

"Look there! the old foxes have come back, out of fear for their cub's safety. Come, we will set it free! " And with these words they untied the string round the cub's neck, and turned its head toward the spot where the old foxes sat; and as the wounded foot was no longer painful, with one bound it dashed to its parents' side and licked them all over for joy, while they seemed to bow their thanks, looking toward the two friends. So, with peace in their hearts, the latter went off to another place, and, choosing a pretty spot, produced the wine bottle and ate their noonday meal; and after a pleasant day, they returned to their homes, and became firmer friends than ever.

Now the man who had rescued the fox's cub was a tradesman in good circumstances: he had three or four agents and two maid-servants, besides men-servants; and altogether he lived in a liberal manner. He was married, and this union had brought him one son, who had reached his tenth year, but had been attacked by a strange disease which defied all the physicians' skill and drugs. At last a famous physician prescribed the liver taken from a live fox, which, as he said, would certainly effect a cure. If that were not forthcoming, the most expensive medicine in the world would not restore the boy to health. When the parents heard this, they were at their wits' end. However, they told the state of the case to a man who lived on the mountains. "Even though our child should die for it, " they said, "we will not ourselves deprive other creatures of their lives; but you, who live among the hills, are sure to hear when your neighbours go out fox-hunting. We don't care what price we might have to pay for a fox's liver; pray, buy one for us at any expense. " So they pressed him to exert himself on their behalf; and he, having promised faithfully to execute the commission, went his way.

In the night of the following day there came a messenger, who announced himself as coming from the person who had undertaken to procure the fox's liver; so the master of the house went out to see him.

"I have come from Mr. So-and-so. Last night the fox's liver that you required fell into his hands; so he sent me to bring it to you. " With these words the messenger produced a small jar, adding, "In a few days he will let you know the price. "

When he had delivered his message, the master of the house was greatly pleased and said, "Indeed, I am deeply grateful for this kindness, which will save my son's life. "

Then the good wife came out, and received the jar with every mark of politeness.

"We must make a present to the messenger. "

"Indeed, sir, I've already been paid for my trouble. "

"Well, at any rate, you must stop the night here. "

"Thank you, sir: I've a relation in the next village whom I have not seen for a long while, and I will pass the night with him; " and so he took his leave, and went away.

The parents lost no time in sending to let the physician know that they had procured the fox's liver. The next day the doctor came and compounded a medicine for the patient, which at once produced a good effect, and there was no little joy in the household. As luck would have it, three days after this the man whom they had commissioned to buy the fox's liver came to the house: so the goodwife hurried out to meet him and welcome him.

"How quickly you fulfilled our wishes, and how kind of you to send at once! The doctor prepared the medicine, and now our boy can get up and walk about the room; and it's all owing to your goodness. "

"Wait a bit! " cried the guest, who did not know what to make of the joy of the two parents. "The commission with which you entrusted me about the fox's liver turned out to be a matter of impossibility, so I came to-day to make my excuses; and now I really can't understand what you are so grateful to me for. "

"We are thanking you, sir, " replied the master of the house, bowing with his hands on the ground, "for the fox's liver which we asked you to procure for us. "

"I really am perfectly unaware of having sent you a fox's liver: there must be some mistake here. Pray inquire carefully into the matter. "

"Well, this is very strange. Four nights ago, a man of some five or six and thirty years of age came with a verbal message from you, to the effect that you had sent him with a fox's liver, which you had just procured, and said that he would come and tell us the price another day. When we asked him to spend the night here, he answered that he would lodge with a relation in the next village, and went away. "

The visitor was more and more lost in amazement, and, leaning his head on one side in deep thought, confessed that he could make nothing of it. As for the husband and wife, they felt quite out of countenance at having thanked a man so warmly for favours of which he denied all knowledge; and so the visitor took his leave and went home.

That night there appeared at the pillow of the master of the house a woman of about one or two and thirty years of age, who said: "I am the fox that lives at such-and-such a mountain. Last spring, when I was taking out my cub to play, it was carried off by some boys, and only saved by your goodness. The desire to requite this kindness pierced me to the quick. At last, when calamity attacked your house, I thought I might be of use to you. Your son's illness could not be cured without a liver taken from a live fox, so to repay your kindness I killed my cub and took out its liver; then its sire, disguising himself as a messenger, brought it to your house. "

And as she spoke, the fox shed tears; and the master of the house, wishing to thank her, moved in bed, upon which his wife awoke and asked him what was the matter; but he too, to her great astonishment, was biting the pillow and weeping bitterly.

"Why are you weeping thus? " asked she.

At last he sat up in bed and said: "Last spring, when I was out on a pleasure excursion, I was the means of saving the life of a fox's cub, as I told you at the time. The other day I told Mr. So-and-so that, although my son were to die before my eyes, I would not be the means of killing a fox on purpose, but asked him, in case he heard of any hunter killing a fox, to buy it for me. How the foxes came to hear of this I don't know; but the foxes to whom I had shown kindness killed their own cub and took out the liver; and the old dog-fox, disguising himself as a messenger from the person to whom we had confided the commission, came here with it. His mate has just been at my pillow-side and told me all about it. Hence it was that, in spite of myself, I was moved to tears. "

When she heard this, the goodwife likewise was blinded by her tears, and for a while they lay lost in thought; but at last, coming to themselves, they lighted the lamp on the shelf on which the family idol stood, and spent the night in reciting prayers and praises, and the next day they published the matter to the household and to their relations and friends. Now, although there are instances of men killing their own children to requite a favour, there is no other example of foxes having done such a thing; so the story became the talk of the whole country.

Now, the boy who had recovered through the efficacy of this medicine selected the prettiest spot on the premises to erect a shrine to Inari Sama, [2] the Fox God, and offered sacrifice to the two old foxes, for whom he purchased the highest rank at the court of the Mikado.

* * * * *

The passage in the tale which speaks of rank being purchased for the foxes at the court of the Mikado is, of course, a piece of nonsense. "The saints who are worshipped in Japan, " writes a native authority, "are men who, in the remote ages, when the country was developing itself, were sages, and by their great and virtuous deeds having earned the gratitude of future generations, received divine honours after their death. How can the Son of Heaven, who is the father and mother of his people, turn dealer in ranks and honours? If rank were a matter of barter, it would cease to be a reward to the virtuous. "

All matters connected with the shrines of the Shintô, or indigenous religion, are confided to the superintendence of the families of Yoshida and Fushimi, Kugés or nobles of the Mikado's court at Kiy'to. The affairs of the Buddhist or imported religion are under the care of the family of Kanjuji. As it is necessary that those who as priests perform the honourable office of serving the gods should be persons of some standing, a certain small rank is procured for them through the intervention of the representatives of the above noble families, who, on the issuing of the required patent, receive as their perquisite a fee, which, although insignificant in itself, is yet of importance to the poor Kugés, whose penniless condition forms a great contrast to the wealth of their inferiors in rank, the Daimios. I believe that this is the only case in which rank can be bought or sold in Japan. In China, on the contrary, in spite of what has been written by Meadows and other admirers of the examination system, a man can be what he pleases by paying for it; and the coveted button, which is nominally the reward of learning and ability, is more often the prize of wealthy ignorance.

The saints who are alluded to above are the saints of the whole country, as distinct from those who for special deeds are locally worshipped.

Touching the remedy of the fox's liver, prescribed in the tale, I may add that there would be nothing strange in this to a person acquainted with the Chinese pharmacopoeia, which the Japanese long exclusively followed, although they are now successfully studying the art of healing as practised in the West. When I was at Peking, I saw a Chinese physician prescribe a decoction of three scorpions for a child struck down with fever; and on another occasion a groom of mine, suffering from dysentery, was treated with acupuncture of the tongue. The art of medicine would appear to be at the present time in China much in the state in which it existed in Europe in the sixteenth century, when the excretions and secretions of all manner of animals, saurians, and venomous snakes and insects, and even live bugs, were administered to patients. "Some physicians, " says Matthiolus, "use the ashes of scorpions, burnt alive, for retention caused by either renal or vesical calculi. But I have myself thoroughly experienced the utility of an oil I make myself, whereof scorpions form a very large portion of the ingredients. If only the region of the heart and all the pulses of the body be anointed with it, it will free the patients from the effects of all kinds of poisons taken by the mouth, corrosive ones excepted. " Decoctions of Egyptian mummies were much commended, and often prescribed with due academical solemnity; and the bones of the human skull, pulverized and administered with oil, were used as a specific in cases of renal calculus. (See Petri Andreæ Matthioli "Opera, " 1574.)

These remarks were made to me by a medical gentleman to whom I mentioned the Chinese doctor's prescription of scorpion tea, and they seem to me so curious that I insert them for comparison's sake.

FOOTNOTES:

[Footnote 1: *Bu.* This coin is generally called by foreigners "ichibu, " which means "one bu. " To talk of "*a hundred ichibus*" is as though a Japanese were to say "*a hundred one shillings.* " Four bus make a *riyo*, or ounce; and any sum above three bus is spoken of as so many riyos and bus—as 101 riyos and three bus equal 407 bus. The bu is worth about 1*s.* 4*d.*]

[Footnote 2: Inari Sama is the title under which was deified a certain mythical personage, called Uga, to whom tradition attributes the honour of having first discovered and cultivated the rice-plant. He is represented carrying a few ears of rice, and is symbolized by a snake guarding a bale of rice grain. The foxes wait upon him, and do his bidding. Inasmuch as rice is the most important and necessary product of Japan, the honours which Inari Sama receives are extraordinary. Almost every house in the country contains somewhere about the grounds a pretty little shrine in his honour; and on a certain day of the second month of the year his feast is celebrated with much beating of drums and other noises, in which the children take a special delight. "On this day, " says the O-Satsuyô, a Japanese cyclopædia, "at Yeddo, where there are myriads upon myriads of shrines to Inari Sama, there are all sorts of ceremonies. Long banners with inscriptions are erected, lamps and lanterns are hung up, and the houses are decked with various dolls and figures; the sound of flutes and drums is heard, and people dance and make holiday according to their fancy. In short, it is the most bustling festival of the Yeddo year. "]

VII

THE BADGER'S MONEY

It is a common saying among men that to forget favours received is the part of a bird or a beast: an ungrateful man will be ill spoken of by all the world. And yet even birds and beasts will show gratitude; so that a man who does not requite a favour is worse even than dumb brutes. Is not this a disgrace?

Once upon a time, in a hut at a place called Namékata, in Hitachi, there lived an old priest famous neither for learning nor wisdom, but bent only on passing his days in prayer and meditation. He had not even a child to wait upon him, but prepared his food with his own hands. Night and morning he recited the prayer "Namu Amida Butsu, "[3] intent upon that alone. Although the fame of his virtue did not reach far, yet his neighbours respected and revered him, and often brought him food and raiment; and when his roof or his walls fell out of repair, they would mend them for him; so for the things of this world he took no thought.

One very cold night, when he little thought any one was outside, he heard a voice calling, "Your reverence! your reverence! " So he rose and went out to see who it was, and there he beheld an old badger standing. Any ordinary man would have been greatly alarmed at the apparition; but the priest, being such as he has been described above, showed no sign of fear, but asked the creature its business. Upon this the badger respectfully bent its knees and said:

"Hitherto, sir, my lair has been in the mountains, and of snow or frost I have taken no heed; but now I am growing old, and this severe cold is more than I can bear. I pray you to let me enter and warm myself at the fire of your cottage, that I may live through this bitter night. "

When the priest heard what a helpless state the beast was reduced to, he was filled with pity and said:

"That's a very slight matter: make haste and come in and warm yourself. "

The badger, delighted with so good a reception, went into the hut, and squatting down by the fire began to warm itself; and the priest, with renewed fervour, recited his prayers and struck his bell before the image of Buddha, looking straight before him.

After two hours the badger took its leave, with profuse expressions of thanks, and went out; and from that time forth it came every night to the hut. As the badger would collect and bring with it dried branches and dead leaves from the hills for firewood, the priest at last became very friendly with it, and got used to its company; so that if ever, as the night wore on, the badger did not arrive, he used to miss it, and wonder why it did not come. When the winter was over, and the springtime came at the end of the second month, the badger gave up its visits, and was no more seen; but, on the return of the winter, the beast resumed its old habit of coming to the hut. When this practice had gone on for ten years, one day the badger said to the priest, "Through your reverence's kindness for all these years, I have been able to pass the winter nights in comfort. Your favours are such that during all my life, and even after my death, I must remember them. What can I do to requite them? If there is anything that you wish for, pray tell me. "

The priest, smiling at this speech, answered: "Being such as I am, I have no desire and no wishes. Glad as I am to hear your kind intentions, there is nothing that I can ask you to do for me. You need feel no anxiety on my account. As long as I live, when the winter comes, you shall be welcome here. " The badger, on hearing this, could not conceal its admiration of the depth of the old man's benevolence; but having so much to be grateful for, it felt hurt at not being able to requite it. As this subject was often renewed between them, the priest at last, touched by the goodness of the badger's heart, said: "Since I have shaven my head, renounced the world, and forsaken the pleasures of this life, I have no desire to gratify, yet I own I should like to possess three riyos in gold. Food and raiment I receive by the favour of the villagers, so I take no heed for those things. Were I to die to-morrow, and attain my wish of being born again into the next world, the same kind folk have promised to meet and bury my body. Thus, although I have no other reason to wish for money, still if I had three riyos I would offer them up at some holy shrine, that masses and prayers might be said for me, whereby I might enter into salvation. Yet I would not get this money by violent or unlawful means; I only think of what might be if I had it. So you see, since you have expressed such kind feelings toward me, I have told you what is on my mind. " When the priest had done speaking, the badger leant its head on one side with a puzzled and anxious look, so much so that the old man was sorry he had expressed a wish which seemed to give the beast trouble, and tried to retract what he had said. "Posthumous honours, after all, are the wish of ordinary men. I, who am a priest, ought not to entertain such thoughts, or to want money; so pray pay no attention to what I have said; " and the badger, feigning assent to what the priest had impressed upon it, returned to the hills as usual.

From that time forth the badger came no more to the hut. The priest thought this very strange, but imagined either that the badger stayed away because it did not like to come without the money, or that it had been killed in an attempt to steal it; and he blamed himself for having added to his sins for no purpose, repenting when it was too late: persuaded, however, that the badger must have been killed, he passed his time in putting up prayers upon prayers for it.

After three years had gone by, one night the old man heard a voice near his door calling out, "Your reverence! your reverence! "

As the voice was like that of the badger, he jumped up as soon as he heard it, and ran to open the door; and there, sure enough, was the badger. The priest, in great delight, cried out: "And so you are safe and sound, after all! Why have you been so long without coming here? I have been expecting you anxiously this long while. "

So the badger came into the hut and said: "If the money which you required had been for unlawful purposes, I could easily have procured as much as ever you might have wanted; but when I heard that it was to be offered to a temple for masses for your soul, I thought that, if I were to steal the hidden treasure of some other man, you could not apply to a sacred purpose money which had been obtained at the expense of his sorrow. So I went to the island of Sado, [4] and gathering the sand and earth which had been cast away as worthless by the miners, fused it afresh in the fire; and at this work I spent months and days. " As the badger finished speaking, the priest looked at the money which it had produced, and sure enough he saw that it was bright and new and clean; so he took the money, and received it respectfully, raising it to his head.

"And so you have had all this toil and labour on account of a foolish speech of mine? I have obtained my heart's desire, and am truly thankful. "

As he was thanking the badger with great politeness and ceremony, the beast said: "In doing this I have but fulfilled my own wish; still I hope that you will tell this thing to no man. "

"Indeed, " replied the priest, "I cannot choose but tell this story. For if I keep this money in my poor hut, it will be stolen by thieves: I must either give it to some one to keep for me, or else at once offer it up at the temple. And when I do this, when people see a poor old priest with a sum of money quite unsuited to his station, they will think it very suspicious, and I shall have to tell the tale as it occurred; but I shall say that the badger that gave me the money has ceased coming to my hut, you need not fear being waylaid, but can come, as of old, and shelter yourself from the cold. " To this the badger nodded assent; and as long as the old priest lived, it came and spent the winter nights with him.

From this story, it is plain that even beasts have a sense of gratitude: in this quality dogs excel all other beasts. Is not the story of the dog of Totoribé Yorodzu written in the Annals of Japan? I[5] have heard that many anecdotes of this nature have been collected and printed in a book, which I have not yet seen; but as the facts which I have recorded relate to a badger, they appear to me to be passing strange.

FOOTNOTES:

[Footnote 3: A Buddhist prayer, in which something approaching to the sounds of the original Sanscrit has been preserved. The meaning of the prayer is explained as, "Save us, eternal Buddha'" Many even of the priests who repeat it know it only as a formula, without understanding it.]

[Footnote 4: An island on the west coast of Japan, famous for its gold mines.]

[Footnote 5: The author of the tale.]

VIII

WHY BROTHER BEAR HAS NO TAIL

"I 'clar' ter gracious, honey, " Uncle Remus exclaimed one night, as the little boy ran in, "you sholy ain't chaw'd yo' vittles. Hit ain't bin no time, skacely, sence de supper-bell rung, en ef you go on dis a-way, you'll des nat'ally pe'sh yo'se'f out. "

"Oh, I wasn't hungry, " said the little boy. "I had something before supper, and I wasn't hungry anyway. "

The old man looked keenly at the child, and presently he said:

"De ins en de outs er dat kinder talk all come ter de same p'int in my min'. Youer bin a-cuttin' up at de table, en Mars John, he tuck'n sont you 'way fum dar, en w'iles he think youer off some'er a-snifflin' en a-feelin' bad, yer you is a-high-primin' 'roun' des lak you done had mo' supper dan de King er Philanders. "

Before the little boy could inquire about the King of Philanders he heard his father calling him. He started to go out, but Uncle Remus motioned him back.

"Des set right whar you is, honey—des set right still. "

Then Uncle Remus went to the door and answered for the child; and a very queer answer it was—one that could be heard half over the plantation:

"Mars John, I wish you en Miss Sally be so good ez ter let dat chile 'lone. He down yer cryin' he eyes out, en he ain't boddern' 'long er nobody in de roun' worl'. "

Uncle Remus stood in the door a moment to see what the reply would be, but he heard none. Thereupon he continued, in the same loud tone:

"I ain't bin use ter no sich gwines on in Ole Miss time, en I ain't gwine git use ter it now. Dat I ain't. "

Presently 'Tildy, the house-girl, brought the little boy his supper, and the girl was no sooner out of hearing than the child swapped it with Uncle Remus for a roasted yam, and the enjoyment of both seemed to be complete.

"Uncle Remus, " said the little boy, after a while, "you know I wasn't crying just now. "

"Dat's so, honey, " the old man replied, "but 't wouldn't er bin long 'fo' you would er bin, kaze Mars John bawl out lak a man wa't got a strop in he han', so wa't de diff'unce? "

When they had finished eating, Uncle Remus busied himself in cutting and trimming some sole-leather for future use. His knife was so keen, and the leather fell away from it so smoothly and easily, that the little boy wanted to trim some himself. But to this Uncle Remus would not listen.

"'Tain't on'y chilluns w'at got de consate er doin' eve'ything dey see yuther folks do. Hit's grown folks w'at oughter know better, " said the old man. "Dat's des de way Brer B'ar git his tail broke off smick-smack-smoove, en down ter dis day he be funnies'-lookin' creetur w'at wobble on top er dry groun'. "

Instantly the little boy forgot all about Uncle Remus's sharp knife.

"Hit seem lak dat in dem days Brer Rabbit en Brer Tarrypin done gone in cohoots fer ter outdo de t'er creeturs. One time Brer Rabbit tuck'n make a call on Brer Tarrypin, but w'en he git ter Brer Tarrypin house, he year talk fum Miss Tarrypin dat her ole man done gone fer ter spen' de day wid Mr. Mud-Turkle, w'ich dey wuz blood kin. Brer Rabbit he put out atter Brer Tarrypin, en w'en he got ter Mr. Mud-Turkle house, dey all sot up, dey did, en tole tales, en den w'en twelf er' clock come dey had crawfish fer dinner, en dey 'joy deyse'f right erlong. Atter dinner dey went down ter Mr. Mud-Turkle mill-pon, ' en w'en dey git dar Mr. Mud-Turkle en Brer Tarrypin dey 'muse deyse'f, dey did, wid slidin' fum de top uv a big slantin' rock down inter de water.

"I'speck you moughter seen rocks in de water 'fo' now, whar dey git green en slipp'y, " said Uncle Remus.

The little boy had not only seen them, but had found them to be very dangerous to walk upon, and the old man continued:

"Well, den, dish yer rock wuz mighty slick en mighty slantin'. Mr. Mud-Turkle, he'd crawl ter de top, en tu'n loose, en go a-sailin' down inter de water—*kersplash!* Ole Brer Tarrypin, he'd foller atter, en slide down inter de water—*kersplash!* Ole Brer Rabbit, he sot off, he did, en praise um up.

"W'iles dey wuz a-gwine on dis a-way, a-havin' der fun, en 'joyin' deyse'f, yer come ole Brer B'ar. He year um laffin' en holl'in', en he hail um.

"'Heyo, folks! W'at all dis? Ef my eye ain't 'ceive me, dish yer's Brer Rabbit, en Brer Tarrypin, en ole Unk' Tommy Mud-Turkle, ' sez Brer B'ar, sezee.

"'De same, ' sez Brer Rabbit, sezee, 'en yer we is 'joyin' de day dat passes des lak dey wa'n't no hard times. '

"'Well, well, well! ' sez ole Brer B'ar, sezee, 'a-slippin' en a-slidin' en makin' free! En w'at de matter wid Brer Rabbit dat he ain't j'inin' in? ' sezee.

"Ole Brer Rabbit he wink at Brer Tarrypin, en Brer Tarrypin he hunch Mr. Mud-Turkle, en den Brer Rabbit he up'n 'low, he did:

"'My goodness, Brer B'ar! you can't 'speck a man fer ter slip en slide de whole blessid day, kin you? I done had my fun, en now I'm a-settin' out yer lettin' my cloze dry. Hit's tu'n en tu'n about wid me en deze gents w'en dey's any fun gwine on, ' sezee.

"'Maybe Brer B'ar might jine in wid us, ' sez Brer Tarrypin, sezee.

"Brer Rabbit he des holler en laff.

"'Shoo! ' sezee, 'Brer B'ar foot too big en he tail too long fer ter slide down dat rock, ' sezee.

"Dis kinder put Brer B'ar on he mettle, en he up'n 'spon', he did:

"'Maybe dey is, en maybe dey ain't, yit I ain't a-feared ter try. '

"Wid dat de yuthers tuck'n made way fer 'im, en ole Brer B'ar he git up on de rock he did, en squot down on he hunkers, en quile he tail und' 'im, en start down. Fus' he go sorter slow, en he grin lak he feel good; den he go sorter peart, en he grin lak he feel bad; den he go mo' pearter, en he grin lak he skeerd; den he strack de slick part, en, gentermens! he swaller de grin en fetch a howl dat moughter bin yeard a mile, en he hit de water lak a chimbly a-fallin'.

"You kin gimme denial, " Uncle Remus continued after a little pause, "but des ez sho' ez you er settin' dar, w'en Brer B'ar slick'd up en flew down dat rock, he break off he tail right smick-smack-smoove, en mo'n dat, w'en he make his disappear'nce up de big road, Brer Rabbit holler out:

"'Brer B'ar! —O Brer B'ar! I year tell dat flaxseed poultices is mighty good fer so' places! '

"Yit Brer B'ar ain't look back. "

IX

THE ORIGIN OF RUBIES

There was a certain king who died leaving four sons behind him with his queen. The queen was passionately fond of the youngest of the princes. She gave him the best robes, the best horses, the best food, and the best furniture. The other three princes became exceedingly jealous of their youngest brother, and, conspiring against him and their mother, made them live in a separate house, and took possession of the estate. Owing to overindulgence, the youngest prince had become very wilful. He never listened to any one, not even to his mother, but had his own way in everything. One day he went with his mother to bathe in the river. A large boat was riding there at anchor. None of the boatmen were in it. The prince went into the boat, and told his mother to come into it. His mother besought him to get down from the boat, as it did not belong to him. But the prince said, "No, mother I am not coming down; I mean to go on a voyage, and if you wish to come with me, then delay not but come up at once, or I shall be off in a trice. " The queen besought the prince to do no such thing, but to come down instantly. But the prince gave no heed to what she said, and began to take up the anchor. The queen went up into the boat in great haste; and the moment she was on board the boat started, and falling into the current passed on swiftly like an arrow. The boat went on and on till it reached the sea. After it had gone many furlongs into the open sea, the boat came near a whirlpool where the prince saw a great many rubies of monstrous size floating on the waters. Such large rubies no one had ever seen, each being in value equal to the wealth of seven kings. The prince caught hold of half-a-dozen of those rubies, and put them on board. His mother said, "Darling, don't take up those red balls; they must belong to somebody who has been shipwrecked, and we may be taken up as thieves. " At the repeated entreaties of his mother, the prince threw them into the sea, keeping only one tied up in his clothes. The boat then drifted toward the coast, and the queen and the prince arrived at a certain port where they landed.

The port where they landed was not a small place; it was a large city, the capital of a great king. Not far from the palace, the queen and her son hired a hut where they lived. As the prince was yet a boy, he was fond of playing at marbles. When the children of the king came out to play on a lawn before the palace, our young prince joined them.

He had no marbles, but he played with the ruby which he had in his possession. The ruby was so hard that it broke every taw against which it struck. The daughter of the king, who used to watch the games from a balcony of the palace, was astonished to see a brilliant red ball in the hand of the strange lad, and wanted to take possession of it. She told her father that a boy of the street had an uncommonly bright stone in his possession which she must have or else she would starve herself to death. The king ordered his servants to bring to him the lad with that precious stone. When the boy was brought, the king wondered at the largeness and brilliancy of the ruby. He had never seen anything like it. He doubted whether any king of any country in the world possessed so great a treasure. He asked the lad where he had got it. The lad replied that he got it from the sea. The king offered a thousand rupees for the ruby, and the lad, not knowing its value, readily parted with it for that sum. He went with the money to his mother, who was not a little frightened, thinking that her son had stolen the money from some rich man's house. She became quiet, however, on being assured that the money was given to him by the king in exchange for the red ball which he had picked up in the sea.

The king's daughter, on getting the ruby put it in her hair, and, standing before her pet parrot, said to the bird, "Oh, my darling parrot, don't I look very beautiful with this ruby in my hair? " The parrot replied, "Beautiful! you look quite hideous with it! What princess ever puts only one ruby in her hair? It would be somewhat feasible if you had two at least. " Stung with shame at the reproach cast in her teeth by the parrot, the princess went into the grief-chamber of the palace, and would neither eat nor drink. The king was not a little concerned when he heard that his daughter had gone into the grief-chamber. He went to her, and asked her the cause of her grief. The princess told the king what her pet parrot had said, and added, "Father, if you do not procure for me another ruby like this, I'll put an end to my life by mine own hands. " The king was overwhelmed with grief. Where was he to get another ruby like it? He doubted whether another like it could be found in the whole world. He ordered the lad who had sold the ruby, to be brought into his presence. "Have you, young man, " asked the king, "another ruby like the one you sold me? " The lad replied: "No, I have not got one. Why, do you want another? I can give you lots, if you wish to have them. They are to be found in a whirlpool in the sea, far, far away. I can go and fetch some for you. " Amazed at the lad's reply, the king offered rich rewards for procuring only another ruby of the same sort.

The lad went home and said to his mother that he must go to sea again to fetch some rubies for the king. The woman was quite frightened at the idea, and begged him not to go. But the lad was resolved on going, and nothing could prevent him from carrying out his purpose. He accordingly went alone on board that same vessel which had brought him and his mother, and set sail. He reached the whirlpool, from near which he had formerly picked up the rubies. This time, however, he determined to go to the exact spot whence the rubies were coming out. He went to the centre of the whirlpool, where he saw a gap reaching to the bottom of the ocean. He dived into it, leaving his boat to wheel round the whirlpool. When he reached the bottom of the ocean he saw there a beautiful palace. He went inside. In the central room of the palace there was the god Siva, with his eyes closed, and absorbed apparently in intense meditation. A few feet above Siva's head was a platform, on which lay a young lady of exquisite beauty. The prince went to the platform and saw that the head of the lady was separated from her body. Horrified at the sight, he did not know what to make of it. He saw a stream of blood trickling from the severed head, falling upon the matted head of Siva, and running into the ocean in the form of rubies. After a little two small rods, one of silver and one of gold, which were lying near the head of the lady, attracted his eyes. As he took up the rods in his hands, the golden rod accidentally fell upon the head, on which the head immediately joined itself to the body, and the lady got up. Astonished at the sight of a human being, the lady asked the prince who he was and how he had got there. After hearing the story of the prince's adventures, the lady said, "Unhappy young man, depart instantly from this place; for when Siva finishes his meditations he will turn you to ashes by a single glance of his eyes. " The young man, however, would not go except in her company, as he was over head and ears in love with the beautiful lady. At last they both contrived to run away from the palace, and coming up to the surface of the ocean they climbed into the boat near the centre of the whirlpool, and sailed away toward land, having previously laden the vessel with a cargo of rubies. The wonder of the prince's mother at seeing the beautiful damsel may be well imagined. Early next morning the prince sent a basin full of big rubies, through a servant. The king was astonished beyond measure. His daughter, on getting the rubies, resolved on marrying the wonderful lad who had made a present of them to her. Though the prince had a wife, whom he had brought up from the depths of the ocean, he consented to have a second wife. They were accordingly married, and lived happily for years, begetting sons and daughters.

> Here my story endeth,
> The Natiya-thorn withereth, etc.

X

LONG, BROAD, AND SHARPSIGHT

There was a king, who was already old, and had but one son. Once upon a time he called this son to him and said to him: "My dear son! you know that old fruit falls to make room for other fruit. My head is already ripening, and maybe the sun will soon no longer shine upon it; but before you bury me, I should like to see your wife, my future daughter. My son, marry! " The prince said: "I would gladly, father, do as you wish; but I have no bride, and don't know any. " The old king put his hand into his pocket, took out a golden key and showed it to his son, with the words, "go up into the tower, to the top story, look round there, and then tell me which you fancy. " The prince went without delay. Nobody within the memory of man had been up there or had ever heard what was up there.

When he got up to the last story, he saw in the ceiling a little iron door like a trap-door. It was closed. He opened it with the golden key, lifted it, and went up above it. There was a large circular room. The ceiling was blue like the sky on a clear night, and silver stars glittered on it, the floor was a carpet of green silk, and around in the wall were twelve high windows in golden frames, and in each window on crystal glass was a damsel painted with the colours of the rainbow, with a royal crown on her head, in each window a different one in a different dress, each handsomer than the other, and it was a wonder that the prince did not let his eyes dwell upon them. When he had gazed at them with astonishment, the damsels began to move as if they were alive, looked down upon him, smiled, and did everything but speak.

Now the prince observed that one of the twelve windows was covered with a white curtain; he drew the curtain to see what was behind it. There there was a damsel in a white dress, girt with a silver girdle, with a crown of pearls on her head; she was the most beautiful of all, but was sad and pale, as if she had risen from the grave. The prince stood long before the picture, as if he had made a discovery, and as he thus gazed, his heart pained him, and he cried, "This one will I have, and no other. " As he said the words the damsel bowed her head, blushed like a rose, and that instant all the pictures disappeared.

When he went down and related to his father what he had seen and which damsel he had selected, the old king became sad, bethought himself, and said: "You have done ill, my son, in uncovering what was curtained over, and have placed yourself in great danger on account of those words. That damsel is in the power of a wicked wizard, and kept captive in an iron castle; of all who have attempted to set her free, not one has hitherto returned. But what's done cannot be undone; the plighted word is a law. Go! try your luck, and return home safe and sound! "

The prince took leave of his father, mounted his horse, and rode away in search of his bride. It came to pass that he rode through a vast forest, and through the forest he rode on and on till he lost the road. And as he was wandering with his horse in thickets and amongst rocks and morasses, not knowing which way to turn, he heard somebody shout behind him, "Hi! stop! " The prince looked round, and saw a tall man hastening after him. "Stop and take me with you, and take me into your service, and you won't regret it! " "Who are you, " said the prince, "and what can you do? " "My name is Long, and I can extend myself. Do you see a bird's nest in that pine yonder? I will bring you the nest down without having to climb up. "

Long then began to extend himself; his body grew rapidly till it was as tall as the pine; he then reached the nest, and in a moment contracted himself again and gave it to the prince. "You know your business well, but what's the use of birds' nests to me, if you can't conduct me out of this forest? "

"Ahem! that's an easy matter, " said Long, and began to extend himself till he was thrice as high as the highest fir in the forest, looked round, and said: "Here on this side we have the nearest way out of the forest. " He then contracted himself, took the horse by the bridle, and before the prince had any idea of it, they were beyond the forest. Before them was a long and wide plain, and beyond the plain tall gray rocks like the walls of a large town, and mountains overgrown with forest trees.

"Yonder, sir, goes my comrade! " said Long, and pointed suddenly to the plain; "you should take him also into your service; I believe he would serve you well. " "Shout to him, and call him hither, that I may see what he is good for. " "It is a little too far, sir, " said Long; "he would hardly hear me, and it would take a long time before he came, because he has a great deal to carry. I'll jump after him instead. " Then Long again extended himself to such a height that his head plunged into the clouds, made two or three steps, took his comrade by the arm, and placed him before the prince. He was a short, thick-set fellow, with a paunch like a sixty-four-gallon cask. "Who are you? " demanded the prince, "and what can you do? " "My name, sir, is Broad; I can widen myself. " "Give me a specimen. " "Ride quick, sir, quick, back into the forest! " cried Broad, as he began to blow himself out.

The prince didn't understand why he was to ride away; but seeing that Long made all haste to get into the forest, he spurred his horse and rode full gallop after him. It was high time that he did ride away, or else Broad would have squashed him, horse and all, as his paunch rapidly grew in all directions; it filled everything everywhere, just as if a mountain had rolled up. Broad then ceased to blow himself out, and took himself in again, raising such a wind that the trees in the forest bowed and bent, and became what he was at first. "You have played me a nice trick, " said the prince, "but I shan't find such a fellow every day; come with me. "

They proceeded further. When they approached the rocks, they met a man who had his eyes bandaged with a handkerchief. "Sir, this is our third comrade, " said Long, "you ought to take him also into your service. I'm sure he won't eat his victuals for naught. "

"Who are you? " the prince asked him, "and why are your eyes bandaged? You don't see your way! " "No, sir, quite the contrary! It is just because I see too well that I am obliged to bandage my eyes; I see with bandaged eyes just as well as others with unbandaged eyes; and if I unbandage them I look everything through and through, and when I gaze sharply at anything it catches fire and bursts into flame, and what can't burn splits into pieces. For this reason my name is Sharpsight. " He then turned to a rock opposite, removed the bandage, and fixed his flaming eyes upon it; the rock began to crackle, pieces flew on every side, and in a very short time nothing of it remained but a heap of sand, on which something glittered like fire. Sharpsight went to fetch it, and brought it to the prince. It was pure gold.

"Heigho! you're a fellow that money can't purchase! " said the prince. "He is a fool who wouldn't make use of your services, and if you have such good sight, look and tell me whether it is far to the iron castle, and what is now going on there? " "If you rode by yourself, sir, " answered Sharpsight, "maybe you wouldn't get there within a year; but with us you'll arrive to-day—they're just getting supper ready for us. " "And what is my bride doing? "

> "An iron lattice is before her,
> > In a tower that's high
> > She doth sit and sigh,
> A wizard watch and ward keeps o'er her. "

The prince cried, "Whoever is well disposed, help me to set her free! " They all promised to help him. They guided him among the gray rocks through the breach that Sharpsight had made in them with his eyes, and farther and farther on through rocks, through high mountains and deep forests, and wherever there was any obstacle in the road, forthwith it was removed by the three comrades. And when the sun was declining toward the west, the mountains began to become lower, the forests less dense, and the rocks concealed themselves amongst the heath; and when it was almost on the point of setting, the prince saw not far before him an iron castle; and when it was actually setting, he rode by an iron bridge to the gate, and as soon as it had set, up rose the iron bridge of itself, the gate closed with a single movement, and the prince and his companions were captives in the iron castle.

When they had looked round the court, the prince put his horse up in the stable, where everything was ready for it, and then they went into the castle. In the court, in the stable, in the castle hall, and in the rooms, they saw in the twilight many richly-dressed people, gentlemen and servants, but not one of them stirred—they were all turned to stone. They went through several rooms, and came into the supper-room. This was brilliantly lighted up, and in the midst was a table, and on it plenty of good meats and drinks, and covers were laid for four persons. They waited and waited, thinking that some one would come: but when nobody came for a long time, they sat down and ate and drank what the palate fancied.

When they had done eating, they looked about to find where to sleep. Thereupon the door flew open unexpectedly all at once, and into the room came the wizard; a bent old man in a long black garb, with a bald head, a gray beard down to his knees, and three iron hoops instead of a girdle. By the hand he led a beautiful, very beautiful damsel, dressed in white; she had a silver girdle round her waist, and a crown of pearls on her head, but was pale and sad, as if she had risen from the grave. The prince recognized her at once, sprang forward, and went to meet her; but before he could utter a word the wizard addressed him: "I know for what you have come; you want to take the princess away. Well, be it so! Take her, if you can keep her in sight for three nights, so that she doesn't vanish from you. If she vanishes, you will be turned into stone as well as your three servants; like all who have come before you. " He then motioned the princess to a seat and departed.

The prince could not take his eyes off the princess, so beautiful was she. He began to talk to her, and asked her all manner of questions, but she neither answered nor smiled, nor looked at any one more than if she had been of marble. He sat down by her, and determined not to sleep all night long lest she should vanish from him, and, to make surer, Long extended himself like a strap, and wound himself round the whole room along the wall; Broad posted himself in the doorway, swelled himself up, and stopped it up so tight that not even a mouse could have slipped through; while Sharpsight placed himself against a pillar in the midst of the room on the look-out. But after a time they all began to nod, fell asleep, and slept the whole night, just as if the wizard had thrown them into the water.

In the morning, when it began to dawn, the prince was the first to wake, but—as if a knife had been thrust into his heart—the princess was gone! He forthwith awoke his servants, and asked what was to be done. "Never mind, sir, " said Sharpsight, and looked sharply out through the window, "I see her already. A hundred miles hence is a forest, in the midst of the forest an old oak, and on the top of the oak an acorn, and she is that acorn. " Long immediately took him on his shoulders, extended himself, and went ten miles at a step, while Sharpsight showed him the way.

No more time elapsed than would have been wanted to move once round a cottage before they were back again, and Long delivered the acorn to the prince. "Sir, let it fall on the ground. " The prince let it fall and that moment the princess stood beside him. And when the sun began to show itself beyond the mountains, the folding doors flew open with a crash, and the wizard entered the room and smiled spitefully; but when he saw the princess he frowned, growled, and bang! one of the iron hoops which he wore splintered and sprang off him. He then took the damsel by the hand and led her away.

The whole day after the prince had nothing to do but walk up and down the castle, and round about the castle, and look at the wonderful things that were there. It was everywhere as if life had been lost in a single moment. In one hall he saw a prince, who held in both hands a brandished sword, as if he intended to cleave somebody in twain; but the blow never fell: he had been turned into stone. In one chamber was a knight turned into stone, just as if he had been fleeing from some one in terror, and, stumbling on the threshold, had taken a downward direction, but not fallen. Under the chimney sat a servant, who held in one hand a piece of roast meat, and with the other lifted a mouthful toward his mouth, which never reached it; when it was just in front of his mouth, he had also been turned to stone. Many others he saw there turned to stone, each in the position in which he was when the wizard said, "Be turned into stone. " He likewise saw many fine horses turned to stone, and in the castle and round the castle all was desolate and dead; there were trees, but without leaves; there were meadows, but without grass; there was a river but it did not flow; nowhere was there even a singing bird, or a flower, the offspring of the ground, or a white fish in the water.

Morning, noon, and evening the prince and his companions found good and abundant entertainment in the castle; the viands came of themselves, the wine poured itself out. After supper the folding doors opened again, and the wizard brought in the princess for the prince to guard. And although they all determined to exert themselves with all their might not to fall asleep, yet it was of no use, fall asleep again they did. And when the prince awoke at dawn and saw the princess had vanished, he jumped up and pulled Sharpsight by the arm, "Hey! get up, Sharpsight, do you know where the princess is? " He rubbed his eyes, looked, and said: "I see her. There's a mountain two hundred miles off, and in the mountain a rock, and in the rock a precious stone, and she's that precious stone. If Long carries me thither, we shall obtain her. "

Long took him at once on his shoulders, extended himself, and went twenty miles at a step. Sharpsight fixed his flaming eyes on the mountain, the mountain crumbled, and the rock in it split into a thousand pieces, and amongst them glittered the precious stone. They took it up and brought it to the prince, and when he let it fall on the ground, the princess again stood there. When afterward the wizard came and saw her there, his eyes flashed with spite, and bang! again an iron hoop cracked upon him and flew off. He growled and led the princess out of the room.

That day all was again as it had been the day before. After supper the wizard brought the princess in again, looked the prince keenly in the face, and scornfully uttered the words, "It will be seen who's a match for whom; whether you are victorious or I, " and with that he departed. This night they all exerted themselves still more to avoid going to sleep. They wouldn't even sit down, they wanted to walk about all night long, but all in vain; they were bewitched; one fell asleep after the other as he walked and the princess vanished away from them.

In the morning the prince again awoke earliest, and, when he didn't see the princess, woke Sharpsight. "Hey! get up, Sharpsight! look where the princess is! " Sharpsight looked out for a long time. "Oh, sir, " says he, "she is a long way off, a long way off! Three hundred miles off is a black sea, and in the midst of the sea a shell on the bottom, and in the shell is a gold ring, and she's the ring. But never mind! we shall obtain her, but to-day Long must take Broad with him as well; we shall want him. " Long took Sharpsight on one shoulder, and Broad on the other, and went thirty miles at a step. When they came to the black sea, Sharpsight showed him where he must reach into the water for the shell. Long extended his hand as far as he could, but could not reach the bottom.

"Wait, comrades! wait only a little and I'll help you, " said Broad, and swelled himself out as far as his paunch would stretch; he then lay down on the shore and drank. In a very short time the water fell so low that Long easily reached the bottom and took the shell out of the sea. Out of it he extracted the ring, took his comrades on his shoulders and hastened back. But on the way he found it a little difficult to run with Broad, who had half a sea of water inside him, so he cast him from his shoulder on to the ground in a wide valley. Thump he went like a sack let fall from a tower, and in a moment the whole valley was under water like a vast lake. Broad himself barely crawled out of it.

Meanwhile the prince was in great trouble in the castle. The dawn began to display itself over the mountains, and his servants had not returned; the more brilliantly the rays ascended, the greater was his anxiety; a deadly perspiration came out upon his forehead. Soon the sun showed itself in the east like a thin slip of flame—and then with a loud crash the door flew open, and on the threshold stood the wizard. He looked round the room, and seeing the princess was not there, laughed a hateful laugh and entered the room. But just at that moment, pop! the window flew in pieces, the gold ring fell on the floor, and in an instant there stood the princess again. Sharpsight, seeing what was going on in the castle, and in what danger his master was, told Long. Long made a step, and threw the ring through the window into the room. The wizard roared with rage till the castle quaked, and then, bang! went the third iron hoop that was round his waist, and sprang off him; the wizard turned into a raven, and flew out and away through the shattered window.

Then, and not till then, did the beautiful damsel speak and thank the prince for setting her free, and blushed like a rose. In the castle and round the castle everything became alive again at once. He who was holding in the hall the outstretched sword, swung it into the air, which whistled again, and then returned it to its sheath; he who was stumbling on the threshold, fell on the ground, but immediately got up again and felt his nose to see whether it was still entire; he who was sitting under the chimney put the piece of meat into his mouth and went on eating; and thus everybody completed what he had begun doing, and at the point where he had left off. In the stables the horses merrily stamped and snorted, the trees round the castle became green like periwinkles, the meadows were full of variegated flowers, high in the air warbled the skylark, and abundance of small fishes appeared in the clear river. Everywhere was life, everywhere enjoyment.

Meanwhile a number of gentlemen assembled in the room where the prince was, and all thanked him for their liberation. But he said: "You have nothing to thank me for; if it had not been for my trusty servants Long, Broad, and Sharpsight, I too, should have been what you were. " He then immediately started on his way home to the old king, his father, with his bride and servants. On the way they met Broad and took him with them.

The old king wept for joy at the success of his son; he had thought he would return no more. Soon afterward there was a grand wedding, the festivities of which lasted three weeks; all the gentlemen that the prince had liberated were invited. After the wedding Long, Broad, and Sharpsight announced to the young king that they were going again into the world to look for work. The young king tried to persuade them to stay with him. "I will give you everything you want, as long as you live, " said he; "you needn't work at all. " But they didn't like such an idle life, took leave of him, went away, and have been ever since knocking about somewhere or other in the world.

XI

INTELLIGENCE AND LUCK

Once upon a time Luck met Intelligence on a garden-seat. "Make room for me! " said Luck. Intelligence was then as yet inexperienced, and didn't know who ought to make room for whom. He said: "Why should I make room for you? you're no better than I. " "He's the better man, " answered Luck, "who performs most. See you there yon peasant's son who's ploughing in the field? Enter into him, and if he gets on better through you than through me, I'll always submissively make way for you, whensoever and wheresoever we meet. " Intelligence agreed, and entered at once into the ploughboy's head. As soon as the ploughboy felt that he had intelligence in his head, he began to think: "Why must I follow the plough to the day of my death? I can go somewhere else and make my fortune more easily. " He left off ploughing, put up the plough, and drove home. "Daddy, " says he, "I don't like this peasant's life; I'd rather learn to be a gardener. " His father said: "What ails you, Vanek? have you lost your wits? " However, he bethought himself and said: "Well, if you will, learn, and God be with you! Your brother will be heir to the cottage after me. " Vanek lost the cottage, but he didn't care for that, but went and put himself apprentice to the king's gardener. For every little that the gardener showed him, Vanek comprehended ever so much more. Ere long he didn't even obey the gardener's orders as to how he ought to do anything, but did everything his own way. At first the gardener was angry, but, seeing everything thus getting on better, he was content. "I see that you've more intelligence than I, " said he, and henceforth let Vanek garden as he thought fit. In no long space of time Vanek made the garden so beautiful that the king took great delight in it, and frequently walked in it with the queen and with his only daughter.

The princess was a very beautiful damsel, but ever since she was twelve years old she had ceased speaking, and no one ever heard a single word from her. The king was much grieved, and caused a proclamation to be made that whoever should bring it to pass that she should speak again, should be her husband. Many young kings, princes, and other great lords announced themselves one after the other, but all went away as they had come; no one succeeded in causing her to speak. "Why shouldn't I try my luck? " thought Vanek; "who knows whether I mayn't succeed in bringing her to

50

answer when I ask her a question? " He at once caused himself to be announced at the palace, and the king and his councillors conducted him into the room where the princess was. The king's daughter had a pretty little dog, and was very fond of him, because he was so clever, understanding everything that she wanted. When Vanek went into the room with the king and his councillors, he made as if he didn't even see the princess, but turned to the dog and said: "I have heard, doggie, that you are very clever, and I come to you for advice. We are three companions in travel, a sculptor, a tailor, and myself. Once upon a time we were going through a forest and were obliged to pass the night in it. To be safe from wolves, we made a fire, and agreed to keep watch one after the other. The sculptor kept watch first, and for amusement to kill time took a log and carved a damsel out of it. When it was finished, he woke the tailor to keep watch in his turn. The tailor, seeing the wooden damsel, asked what it meant. 'As you see, ' said the sculptor, 'I was weary, and didn't know what to do with myself, so I carved a damsel out of a log; if you find time hang heavy on your hands, you can dress her. ' The tailor at once took out his scissors, needle and thread, cut out the clothes, stitched away, and, when they were ready, dressed the damsel in them. He then called me to come and keep watch. I, too, asked him what the meaning of all this was. 'As you see, ' said the tailor, 'the sculptor found time hang heavy on his hands and carved a damsel out of a log, and I for the same reason clothed her; and if you find time hanging on your hands, you can teach her to speak. ' And by morning dawn I had actually taught her to speak. But in the morning when my companions woke up, each wanted to possess the damsel. The sculptor said, 'I made her; ' the tailor, 'I clothed her. ' I, too, maintained my right. Tell me, therefore, doggie, to which of us the damsel belongs. " The dog said nothing, but instead of the dog the princess replied: "To whom can she belong but to yourself? What's the good of the sculptor's damsel without life? What's the good of the tailor's dressing without speech? You gave her the best gift, life and speech, and therefore she by right belongs to you. " "You have passed your own sentence, " said Vanek; "I have given you speech again and a new life, and you therefore by right belong to me. " Then said one of the king's councillors: "His Royal Grace will give you a plenteous reward for succeeding in unloosing his daughter's tongue; but you cannot have her to wife, as you are of mean lineage. " The king said: "You are of mean lineage; I will give you a plenteous reward instead of our daughter. " But Vanek wouldn't hear of any other reward, and said: "The king promised without any exception, that whoever caused his daughter to speak

51

again should be her husband. A king's word is law; and if the king wants others to observe his laws, he must first keep them himself. Therefore the king *must* give me his daughter. " "Seize and bind him! " shouted the councillor. "Whoever says the king *must* do anything, offers an insult to his Majesty, and is worthy of death. May it please your Majesty to order this malefactor to be executed with the sword? " The king said: "Let him be executed. " Vanek was immediately bound and led to execution. When they came to the place of execution Luck was there waiting for him, and said secretly to Intelligence: "See how this man has got on through you, till he has to lose his head! Make way, and let me take your place! " As soon as Luck entered Vanek, the executioners sword broke against the scaffold, just as if some one had snapped it; and before they brought him another, up rode a trumpeter on horseback from the city, galloping as swift as a bird, trumpeted merrily, and waved a white flag, and after him came the royal carriage for Vanek. This is what had happened: The princess had told her father at home that Vanek had but spoken the truth, and the king's word ought not to be broken. If Vanek were of mean lineage the king could easily make him a prince. The king said: "You're right; let him be a prince! " The royal carriage was immediately sent for Vanek, and the councillor who had irritated the king against him was executed in his stead. Afterward, when Vanek and the princess were going together in a carriage from the wedding, Intelligence happened to be somewhere on the road, and seeing that he couldn't help meeting Luck, bent his head and slipped on one side, just as if cold water had been thrown upon him. And from that time forth it is said that Intelligence has always given a wide berth to Luck whenever he has had to meet him.

XII

GEORGE WITH THE GOAT

There was a king who had a daughter who never could be induced to laugh; she was always sad. So the king proclaimed that she should be given to any one who could cause her to laugh. There was also a shepherd who had a son named George. He said: "Daddy! I, too, will go to see whether I can make her laugh. I want nothing from you but the goat. " His father said, "Well, go. " The goat was of such a nature that, when her master wished, she detained everybody, and that person was obliged to stay by her.

So he took the goat and went, and met a man who had a foot on his shoulder. George said: "Why have you a foot on your shoulder? " He replied: "If I take it off, I leap a hundred miles. " "Whither are you going? " "I am going in search of service, to see if any one will take me. " "Well, come with us. "

They went on, and again met a man who had a bandage on his eyes. "Why have you a bandage on your eyes? " He answered, "If I remove the bandage, I see a hundred miles. " "Whither are you going? " "I am going in search of service, if you will take me. " "Yes, I'll take you. Come also with me. "

They went on a bit farther, and met another fellow, who had a bottle under his arm, and, instead of a stopper, held his thumb in it. "Why do you hold your thumb there? " "If I pull it out, I squirt a hundred miles, and besprinkle everything that I choose. If you like, take me also into your service; it may be to your advantage and ours too. " George replied: "Well, come, too! "

Afterward they came to the town where the king lived, and bought a silken riband for the goat. They came to an inn, and orders had already been given there beforehand, that when such people came, they were to give them what they liked to eat and drink—the king would pay for all. So they tied the goat with that very riband and placed it in the innkeeper's room to be taken care of, and he put it in the side room where his daughters slept. The innkeeper had three maiden daughters, who were not yet asleep. So Manka said: "Oh! if I, too, could have such a riband! I will go and unfasten it from that goat. " The second, Dodla, said: "Don't; he'll find it out in the morning. " But she went notwithstanding. And when Manka did not return for a long time, the third, Kate, said: "Go, fetch her. " So Dodla went, and gave Manka a pat on the back. "Come, leave it alone! " And now she, too, was unable to withdraw herself from her. So Kate said: "Come, don't unfasten it! " Kate went and gave Dodla a pat on the petticoat; and now she, too, couldn't get away, but was obliged to stay by her.

In the morning George made haste and went for the goat, and led the whole set away—Kate Dodla, and Manka. The innkeeper was still asleep. They went through the village, and the judge looked out of a window and said, "Fie, Kate! what's this? what's this? " He went and took her by the hand, wishing to pull her away, but remained also by her. After this, a cowherd drove some cows through a narrow street, and the bull came rushing round; he stuck fast, and George led him, too, in the procession.

Thus they afterward came in front of the castle, and the servants came out-of-doors; and when they saw such things they went and told the king. "Oh, sire, we have such a spectacle here; we have already had all manner of masquerades, but this has never been here yet. " So they immediately led the king's daughter to the square in front of the castle, and she looked and laughed till the castle shook.

Now they asked him what sort of person he was. He said that he was a shepherd's son, and was named George. They said that it could not be done; for he was of mean lineage, and they could not give him the damsel; but he must accomplish something more for them. He said, "What? " They replied that there was a spring yonder, a hundred miles off; if he brought a goblet of water from it in a minute, then he should obtain the damsel. So George said to the man who had the foot on his shoulder: "You said that if you took the foot down, you could jump a hundred miles. " He replied: "I'll easily do that. " He took the foot down, jumped, and was there. But after this there was only a very little time to spare, and by then he ought to have been back. So George said to the other: "You said that if you removed the bandage from your eyes, you could see a hundred miles. Peep and see what is going on. " "Ah, sir! Goodness gracious! he's fallen asleep! " "That will be a bad job, " said George; "the time will be up. You, third man, you said if you pulled your thumb out, you could squirt a hundred miles; be quick and squirt thither, that he may get up. And you, look whether he is moving, or what. " "Oh, sir, he's

getting up now; he's knocking the dust off; he's drawing the water. "
He then gave a jump, and was there exactly in time.

After this they said that he must perform one task more; that yonder,
in a rock, was a wild beast, a unicorn, of such a nature that he
destroyed a great many of their people; if he cleared him out of the
world he should obtain the damsel. So he took his people and went
into the forest. They came to a firwood. There were three wild beasts,
and three lairs had been formed by wallowing as they lay. Two did
nothing: but the third destroyed the people. So they took some
stones and some pine-cones in their pockets, and climbed up into a
tree; and when the beasts lay down, they dropped a stone down
upon that one which was the unicorn. He said to the next: "Be quiet;
don't butt me. " It said: "I'm not doing anything to you. " Again they
let a stone fall from above upon the unicorn. "Be quiet! you've
already done it to me twice. " "Indeed, I'm doing nothing to you. "
So they attacked each other and fought together. The unicorn wanted
to pierce the second beast through; but it jumped out of the way, and
he rushed so violently after it, that he struck his horn into a tree, and
couldn't pull it out quickly. So they sprang speedily down from the
fir, and the other two beasts ran away and escaped, but they cut off
the head of the third, the unicorn, took it up, and carried it to the
castle.

Now those in the castle saw that George had again accomplished
that task. "What, prithee, shall we do? Perhaps we must after all give
him the damsel! " "No, sire, " said one of the attendants, "that
cannot be; he is too lowborn to obtain a king's daughter! On the
contrary, we must clear him out of the world. " So the king ordered
them to note his words, what he should say. There was a hired
female servant there, and she said to him: "George, it will be evil for
you to-day; they're going to clear you out of the world. " He
answered: "Oh, I'm not afraid. When I was only just twelve years
old, I killed twelve of them at one blow! " But this was the fact: when
his mother was baking a flat-cake, a dozen flies settled upon her, and
he killed them all at a single blow.

When they heard this, they said: "Nothing else will do but we must
shoot him. " So they drew up the soldiers, and said they would hold
a review in his honour, for they would celebrate the wedding in the
square before the castle. Then they conducted him thither, and the
soldiers were already going to let fly at him. But George said to the
man who held his thumb in the bottle in the place of a stopper: "You

said, if you pulled your thumb out, you could besprinkle everything. Pull it out—quick! " "Oh, sir, I'll easily perform that. " So he pulled out his thumb and gave them all such a sprinkling that they were all blind, and not one could see.

So, when they perceived that nothing else was to be done, they told him to go, for they would give him the damsel. Then they gave him a handsome royal robe, and the wedding took place. I, too, was at the wedding; they had music there, sang, ate, and drank; there was meat, there were cheesecakes, and baskets full of everything, and buckets full of strong waters. To-day I went, yesterday I came; I found an egg among the tree-stumps; I knocked it against somebody's head, and gave him a bald place, and he's got it still.

XIII

THE WONDERFUL HAIR

There was a man who was very poor, but so well supplied with children that he was utterly unable to maintain them, and one morning more than once prepared to kill them, in order not to see their misery in dying of hunger, but his wife prevented him. One night a child came to him in his sleep, and said to him: "Man! I see that you are making up your mind to destroy and to kill your poor little children, and I know that you are distressed there at; but in the morning you will find under your pillow a mirror, a red kerchief, and an embroidered pocket-handkerchief; take all three secretly and tell nobody; then go to such a hill; by it you will find a stream; go along it till you come to its fountain-head; there you will find a damsel as bright as the sun, with her hair hanging down over her back. Be on your guard, that the ferocious she-dragon do not coil round you; do not converse with her if she speaks; for if you converse with her, she will poison you, and turn you into a fish or something else, and will then devour you but if she bids you examine her head, examine it, and as you turn over her hair, look, and you will find one hair as red as blood; pull it out and run back again; then, if she suspects and begins to run after you, throw her first the embroidered pocket-handkerchief, then the kerchief, and, lastly, the mirror; then she will find occupation for herself. And sell that hair to some rich man; but don't let them cheat you, for that hair is worth countless wealth; and you will thus enrich yourself and maintain your children. "

When the poor man awoke, he found everything under his pillow, just as the child had told him in his sleep; and then he went to the hill. When there, he found the stream, went on and on alongside of it, till he came to the fountain-head. Having looked about him to see where the damsel was, he espied her above a piece of water, like sunbeams threaded on a needle, and she was embroidering at a frame on stuff, the threads of which were young men's hair. As soon as he saw her, he made a reverence to her, and she stood on her feet and questioned him: "Whence are you, unknown young man? " But he held his tongue. She questioned him again: "Who are you? Why have you come? " and much else of all sorts; but he was as mute as a stone, making signs with his hands, as if he were deaf and wanted help. Then she told him to sit down on her skirt. He did not wait for any more orders, but sat down, and she bent down her head to him, that he might examine it. Turning over the hair of her head, as if to examine it, he was not long in finding that red hair, and separated it from the other hair, pulled it out, jumped off her skirt and ran away back as he best could. She noticed it, and ran at his heels full speed after him. He looked round, and seeing that she was about to overtake him, threw, as he was told, the embroidered pocket-handkerchief on the way, and when she saw the pocket-handkerchief she stooped and began to overhaul it in every direction, admiring the embroidery, till he had got a good way off. Then the damsel placed the pocket-handkerchief in her bosom, and ran after him again. When he saw that she was about to overtake him, he threw the red kerchief, and she again occupied herself, admiring and gazing, till the poor man had again got a good way off. Then the damsel became exasperated, and threw both the pocket-handkerchief and the kerchief on the way, and ran after him in pursuit. Again, when he saw that she was about to overtake him, he threw the mirror. When the damsel came to the mirror, the like of which she had never seen before, she lifted it up, and when she saw herself in it, not knowing that it was herself, but thinking that it was somebody else, she, as it were, fell in love with herself in the mirror, and the man got so far off that she was no longer able to overtake him. When she saw that she could not catch him, she turned back, and the man reached his home safe and sound. After arriving at his home, he showed his wife the hair, and told her all that had happened to him, but she began to jeer and laugh at him. But he paid no attention to her, and went to a town to sell the hair. A crowd of all sorts of people and merchants collected round him; one offered a sequin, another two, and so on, higher and higher, till they came to a hundred gold sequins. Just then the emperor heard of the hair, summoned the man into his presence, and said to him that he would give him a thousand sequins for it, and he sold it to him. What was the hair? The emperor split it in two from top to bottom, and found registered in it in writing many remarkable things, which happened in the olden time since the beginning of the world. Thus the man became rich and lived on with his wife and children. And that child, that came to him in his sleep, was an angel sent by the Lord God, whose will it was to aid the poor man, and to reveal secrets which had not been revealed till then.

XIV

THE DRAGON AND THE PRINCE

There was an emperor who had three sons. One day the eldest son went out hunting, and, when he got outside the town, up sprang a hare out of a bush, and he after it, and hither and thither, till the hare fled into a water-mill, and the prince after it. But it was not a hare, but a dragon, and it waited for the prince and devoured him. When several days had elapsed and the prince did not return home, people began to wonder why it was that he was not to be found. Then the middle son went hunting, and as he issued from the town, a hare sprang out of a bush, and the prince after it, and hither and thither, till the hare fled into the water-mill and the prince after it; but it was not a hare, but a dragon, which waited for and devoured him. When some days had elapsed and the princes did not return, either of them, the whole court was in sorrow. Then the third son went hunting, to see whether he could not find his brothers. When he issued from the town, again up sprang a hare out of a bush, and the prince after it, and hither and thither, till the hare fled into the water-mill. But the prince did not choose to follow it, but went to find other game, saying to himself: "When I return I shall find you. " After thus he went for a long time up and down the hill, but found nothing, and then returned to the water-mill; but when he got there, there was only an old woman in the mill. The prince invoked God in addressing her: "God help you, old woman! " The old woman replied: "God help you, my son! " Then the prince asked her: "Where, old woman, is my hare? " She replied: "My son, that was not a hare, but a dragon. It kills and throttles many people. " Hearing this, the prince was somewhat disturbed, and said to the old woman: "What shall we do now? Doubtless my two brothers also have perished here. " The old woman answered: "They have indeed; but there's no help for it. Go home, my son, lest you follow them. " Then he said to her: "Dear old woman, do you know what? I know that you will be glad to liberate yourself from that pest. " The old woman interrupted him: "How should I not? It captured me, too, in this way, but now I have no means of escape. " Then he proceeded: "Listen well to what I am going to say to you. Ask it whither it goes and where its strength is; then kiss all that place where it tells you its strength is, as if from love, till you ascertain it, and afterward tell me when I come. " Then the prince went off to the palace, and the old woman remained in the water-mill. When the dragon came in, the old woman began to question it: "Where in God's name have you been? Whither do you go so far? You will never tell me whither you go. " The dragon replied: "Well, my dear old woman, I do go far. " Then the old woman began to coax it: "And why do you go so far? Tell me where your strength is. If I knew where your strength is, I don't know what I should do for love; I would kiss all that place. " Thereupon the dragon smiled and said to her: "Yonder is my strength, in that fireplace. " Then the old woman began to fondle and kiss the fireplace, and the dragon on seeing it burst into a laugh and said to her: "Silly old woman, my strength isn't there; my strength is in that tree-fungus in front of the house. " Then the old woman began again to fondle and kiss the tree, and the dragon again laughed, and said to her: "Away, old woman! my strength isn't there. " Then the old woman inquired: "Where is it? " The dragon began to give an account in detail: "My strength is a long way off, and you cannot go thither. Far in another empire under the emperor's city is a lake, in that lake is a dragon, and in that dragon a boar, and in the boar a pigeon, and in that is my strength. " The next morning when the dragon went away from the mill, the prince came to the old woman, and the old woman told him all that she had heard from the dragon. Then he left his home, and disguised himself; he put shepherd's boots to his feet, took a shepherd's staff in his hand, and went into the world. As he went on thus from village to village, and from town to town, at last he came into another empire and into the imperial city, in a lake under which the dragon was. On going into the town he began to inquire who wanted a shepherd. The citizens told him that the emperor did. Then he went straight to the emperor. After he announced himself, the emperor admitted him into his presence, and asked him: "Do you wish to keep sheep? " He replied: "I do, illustrious crown! " Then the emperor engaged him, and began to inform and instruct him: "There is here a lake, and alongside of the lake very beautiful pasture, and when you call the sheep out, they go thither at once, and spread themselves round the lake; but whatever shepherd goes off there, that shepherd returns back no more. Therefore, my son, I tell you, don't let the sheep have their own way and go where *they* will, but keep them where *you* will. " The prince thanked the emperor, got himself ready, and called out the sheep, taking with him, more-over, two hounds that could catch a boar in the open country, and a falcon that could capture any bird, and carrying also a pair of bagpipes. When he called out the sheep he let them go at once to the lake, and when the sheep arrived at the lake, they immediately spread round it, and the prince placed the falcon on a stump, and the hounds and bagpipes under the stump, then tucked up his hose and sleeves, waded into the lake, and began to shout: "Dragon, dragon! come out to single combat with me to-day that we may measure ourselves together, unless you're a woman."[6] The dragon called out in reply, "I will do so now, prince—now!" Erelong behold the dragon! it is large, it is terrible, it is disgusting! When the dragon came out, it seized him by the waist, and they wrestled a summer day till afternoon. But when the heat of afternoon came on, the dragon said: "Let me go, prince, that I may moisten my parched head in the lake, and toss you to the sky." But the prince replied: "Come, dragon, don't talk nonsense; if I had the emperor's daughter to kiss me on the forehead, I would toss you still higher." Thereupon, the dragon suddenly let him go, and went off into the lake. On the approach of evening, he washed and got himself up nicely, placed the falcon on his arm, the hounds behind him, and the bagpipes under his arm, then drove the sheep and went into the town playing on the bagpipes. When he arrived at the town, the whole town assembled as to see a wondrous sight because he had come, whereas previously no shepherd had been able to come from the lake. The next day the prince got ready again, and went with his sheep straight to the lake. But the emperor sent two grooms after him to go stealthily and see what he did, and they placed themselves on a high hill whence they could have a good view. When the shepherd arrived, he put the hounds and bagpipes under the stump and the falcon upon it, then tucked up his hose and sleeves waded into the lake and shouted: "Dragon, dragon! come out to single combat with me, that we may measure ourselves once more together, unless you are a woman!" The dragon replied: "I will do so, prince, now, now!" Erelong, behold the dragon! it was large, it was terrible, it was disgusting! And it seized him by the waist and wrestled with him a summer's day till afternoon. But when the afternoon heat came on, the dragon said: "Let me go, prince, that I may moisten my parched head in the lake, and may toss you to the sky." The prince replied: "Come, dragon, don't talk nonsense; if I had the emperor's daughter to kiss me on the forehead, I would toss you still higher." Thereupon the dragon suddenly left hold of him, and went off into the lake. When night approached the prince drove the sheep as before, and went home playing the bagpipes When he arrived at the town, the whole town was astir and began to wonder because the shepherd came home every evening, which no one had been able to do before. Those two grooms had already arrived at the palace before the prince, and related to the emperor in order everything that they had heard and seen. Now when the emperor saw that the shepherd returned home, he immediately summoned his daughter into his presence and told her all, what it was and how it was. "But, " said he, "to-morrow you must go with the shepherd to the lake and kiss him on the forehead. " When she heard this she burst into tears and began to entreat her father. "You have no one but me, and I am your only daughter, and you don't care about me if I perish. " Then the emperor began to persuade and encourage her: "Don't fear, my daughter; you see we have had so many changes of shepherds, and of all that went out to the lake not one has returned; but *he* had been contending with the dragon for two whole days and it has done him no hurt. I assure you, in God's name, that he is able to overcome the dragon, only go to-morrow with him to see whether he will free us from this mischief which has destroyed so many people. "

When, on the morrow, the day dawned and the sun came forth, up rose the shepherd, up rose the maiden too, to begin to prepare for going to the lake. The shepherd was cheerful, more cheerful than ever, but the emperor's daughter was sad and shed tears. The shepherd comforted her: "Lady sister, I pray you, do not weep, but do what I tell you. When it is time, run up and kiss me, and fear not. " As he went and drove the sheep, the shepherd was thoroughly cheery, and played a merry tune on his bagpipes; but the damsel did nothing but weep as she went beside him, and he several times left off playing and turned toward her: "Weep not, golden one; fear nought. " When they arrived at the lake, the sheep immediately spread round it, and the prince placed the falcon on the stump, and the hounds and bagpipes under it, then tucked up his hose and sleeves, waded into the water, and shouted: "Dragon! dragon! Come out to single combat with me; let us measure ourselves once more, unless you're a woman! " The dragon replied: "I will, prince; now, now! " Erelong, there was the dragon! it was huge, it was terrible, it was disgusting! When it came out, they seized each other by the middle, and wrestled a summer's day till afternoon. But when the afternoon heat came on, the dragon said: "Let me go, prince, that I may moisten my parched head in the lake, and toss you to the skies. " The prince replied: "Come, dragon, don't talk nonsense; if I had the emperor's daughter to kiss me on the forehead, I would toss you much higher. " When he said this, the emperor's daughter ran up and kissed him on the face, on the eye, and on the forehead. Then he swung the dragon, and tossed it high into the air, and when it fell to the ground it burst into pieces. But as it burst into pieces, out of it sprang a wild boar, and started to run away. But the prince shouted to his shepherd dogs: "Hold it! don't let it go! " and the dogs sprang up and after it, caught it, and soon tore it to pieces. But out of the boar flew a pigeon, and the prince loosed the falcon, and the falcon caught the pigeon and brought it into the prince's hands. The prince said to it: "Tell me now, where are my brothers? " The pigeon replied: "I will; only do me no harm. Immediately behind your father's town is a water-mill, and in the water-mill are three wands that have sprouted up. Cut these three wands up from below, and strike with them upon their root; an iron door will immediately open into a large vault. In that vault are many people, old and young, rich and poor, small and great, wives and maidens, so that you could settle a populous empire; there, too, are your brothers. " When the pigeon had told him all this, the prince immediately wrung its neck.

The emperor had gone out in person, and posted himself on the hill from which the grooms had viewed the shepherd, and he, too, was a spectator of all that had taken place. After the shepherd had thus obtained the dragon's head, twilight began to approach. He washed himself nicely, took the falcon on his shoulder, the hounds behind him, and the bagpipes under his arm, played as he went, drove the sheep, and proceeded to the emperor's palace, with the damsel at his side still in terror. When they came to the town, all the town assembled as to see a wonder. The emperor, who had seen all his heroism from the hill, called him into his presence, and gave him his daughter, went immediately to church, had them married, and held a wedding festival for a week. After this the prince told him who and whence he was, and the emperor and the whole town rejoiced still more. Then, as the prince was urgent to go to his own home, the emperor gave him a large escort, and equipped him for the journey. When they were in the neighbourhood of the water-mill, the prince halted his attendants, went inside, cut up the three wands, and struck the root with them, and the iron door opened at once. In the vault was a vast multitude of people. The prince ordered them to come out one by one, and go whither each would, and stood himself at the door. They came out thus one after another, and lo! there were his brothers also, whom he embraced and kissed. When the whole multitude had come out, they thanked him for releasing and delivering them, and went each to his own home. But he went to his father's house with his brothers and bride, and there lived and reigned to the end of his days.

FOOTNOTES:
[Footnote 6: This is intended as an insult. "Azhdaja, " a dragon, is feminine in Servian.]

XV

THE GOOD CHILDREN

The Lord was angered at mankind, and for three years there was a great famine over all the world; nowhere in the world was even a grain of corn produced, and what people sowed failed to come up from a drought so great that for three years there was not a drop of rain or dew. For one year more people managed to live somehow or other, thrashing up what old corn there was; the rich made money, for corn rose very high. Autumn came. Where anybody had or purchased old seed, they sowed it; and entreated the Lord, hoped in the love of God, if God would give fertility, "if God would forgive our sins. " But it was not so. They did not obtain the love of God. When they cast the seed into the holy earth, that was the last they saw of it; if it germinated somewhat, if it sent up shoots, it withered away close to the ground. Woe! and abundance of it! God's world went on, sorrowed and wept, for now it was manifest that death by hunger was approaching. They somehow got miserably through the winter. Spring came. Where anybody had still any grain, they sowed it. What would come to pass? No blessing was poured forth, for the thought began with wind. Moreover, there was but little snow in the winter, and everything dried up so that the black earth remained as it was. It now came to this—all the world began to perish! The people died; the cattle perished; as misery carried them, so did the people proceed.

There was at that time a powerful emperor in a certain empire: as the young ordinarily cleave to the young, so would he associate only with young men. Whether in council or in office or in the army, there were none but young men; no old men had access to anything anywhere. Well, as young men, unripe in understanding, were the councillors, so was their counsel also unripe. One year passed; a second passed; then, in the third year, they saw that misery was already on every side, that it was already coming to this, that all the world would perish. The young emperor assembled his young council, and they began to advise after their fashion; they advised, they advised, and ah! the resolutions they came to were such that it is a sin even to give an account of their resolutions! Well, the emperor made proclamation after their advice, that all old people were to be drowned, in order that, said he, bread might not be wasted in vain, but there might be a supply of bread for the young;

and that no one should venture, on pain of death, to maintain or harbour any old man. Well, heralds went about throughout the whole country, and promulgated the emperor's command everywhere—yea, brigands seized old people where they chose, and drowned them without mercy.

There were then in a certain place three own brothers, who had an aged father. When they heard of this edict, they told their father; and their father said: "My sons, such is the will of God and the will of the emperor; take me, let me perish at once, only that you, my children, may live on. I am already with one foot in the grave, " "No, our own daddy! we will die, but we will not give you up, " cried the good sons with one voice, and fell upon his neck; "we will keep you; we will take from our own mouths, and will nourish you. "

The three brothers took their aged father, conducted him into their cottage, dug under the raised portion of the floor, made up a bed with sheets and frieze-coats, for straw was scarce, and placed the old man there, brought him a loaf of bread as black as the holy earth, and covered him over with the floor. There the old man abode for two or three months, and his sons brought him clandestinely all they had. The summer passed without harvest, without mowing. September passed too. Autumn passed without joy. Winter passed too. Now came spring; the sun became warm. It was now time to sow, but there was no seed. The world was large, but there was no seed-corn. When one kind was used up, the people sowed others, hoping that there would be a crop; but when they cast it into the holy earth, it rotted there. It seemed as if the end of the world were come.

Then the three sons went to their father, and asked him: "Daddy, what shall we do? It's time to sow. God is now sending showers of rain; the earth is warmed and is crumbling like grits; but of seed there is not a blessed grain, " "Take, my sons, and strip the old roof off the house, and thresh the bundles and sow the chaff. " The lads stripped the house and barn (anyhow, there was nothing in it), and threshed away till the sweat ran from their brows, so that they crushed the bundles as small as poppy-seeds. When they sowed, God gave a blessing; so in a week's time it became green like rue; in a month's time, in two months' time, there was corn, ever so much— ever so much, and all manner of seed was found there: there was rye, there was wheat and barley; yea, maybe, there was also a plant or two of buckwheat and millet. Wherever you went throughout the world there was no corn to be seen; all the plain was overgrown with grasses, steppe-grasses, and thistles, but with *them* was corn like a forest. How people wondered and were astounded! The fame thereof went over the whole world, and the news reached the emperor himself, that in such and such a place there were three own brothers, and with them corn had sprung up for all the world, and so beautiful, never was the like beheld! The emperor ordered the three brothers to appear in the imperial presence.

The brothers heard of it, and smacked the tops of their heads with their hands. "Now it will be amen with us! " They went again to their father. "Daddy! they tell us to appear before the emperor. Advise us, daddy, what to do! " "Go, my sons—what will be, will be; and tell the pure truth before the emperor. " The brothers started off and went to the emperor. The emperor inquired menacingly: "Why, villains, did ye hoard up corn, when there was such a famine that so many people died of hunger? Tell the truth; if not I shall order you to be tortured and racked even unto death. " The brothers related all as it had been, from the beginning to the end. "Now, most gracious emperor, give us over to any torture whatever, or let thy kindness have compassion on us! " The emperor's brow became smooth, his eyes became serene. He then ordered the old father to be brought before him at once, and made him sit beside him close to his throne, and hearkened to his counsel till death, and his sons he rewarded handsomely. He ordered the corn to be collected ear by ear, and to be rubbed out in men's hands; and sent it about for seed-corn in all empires, and from it was produced holy corn for all the world.

XVI

THE DUN HORSE[7]

I

Many years ago there lived in the Pawnee tribe an old woman and her grandson a boy about sixteen years old. These people had no relations and were very poor. They were so poor that they were despised by the rest of the tribe. They had nothing of their own; and always, after the village started to move the camp from one place to another, these two would stay behind the rest, to look over the old camp and pick up anything that the other Indians had thrown away as worn out or useless. In this way they would sometimes get pieces of robes, wornout moccasins with holes in them, and bits of meat.

Now, it happened one day, after the tribe had moved away from the camp, that this old woman and her boy were following along the trail behind the rest, when they came to a miserable old wornout dun horse, which they supposed had been abandoned by some Indians. He was thin and exhausted, was blind of one eye, had a bad sore back, and one of his forelegs was very much swollen. In fact, he was so worthless that none of the Pawnees had been willing to take the trouble to try to drive him along with them. But when the old woman and her boy came along, the boy said, "Come now, we will take this old horse, for we can make him carry our pack. " So the old woman put her pack on the horse, and drove him along, but he limped and could only go very slowly.

II

The tribe moved up on the North Platte, until they came to Court House Rock. The two poor Indians followed them, and camped with the others. One day while they were here, the young men who had been sent out to look for buffalo, came hurrying into camp and told the chiefs that a large herd of buffalo were near, and that among them was a spotted calf.

The Head Chief of the Pawnees had a very beautiful daughter, and when he heard about the spotted calf, he ordered his old crier to go about through the village and call out that the man who killed the spotted calf should have his daughter for his wife. For a spotted robe is *ti-war'-uks-ti*—big medicine.

The buffalo were feeding about four miles from the village, and the chiefs decided that the charge should be made from there. In this way, the man who had the fastest horse would be the most likely to kill the calf. Then all the warriors and the young men picked out their best and fastest horses, and made ready to start. Among those who prepared for the charge was the poor boy on the old dun horse. But when they saw him, all the rich young braves on their fast horses pointed at him and said, "Oh, see; there is the horse that is going to catch the spotted calf; " and they laughed at him, so that the poor boy was ashamed, and rode off to one side of the crowd, where he could not hear their jokes and laughter.

When he had ridden off some little way the horse stopped and turned his head round, and spoke to the boy. He said, "Take me down the creek, and plaster me all over with mud. Cover my head and neck and body and legs. " When the boy heard the horse speak, he was afraid; but he did as he was told. Then the horse said, "Now mount, but do not ride back to the warriors, who laugh at you because you have such a poor horse. Stay right here until the word is given to charge. " So the boy stayed there.

And presently all the fine horses were drawn up in line and pranced about, and were so eager to go that their riders could hardly hold them in; and at last the old crier gave the word, *"Loo-ah! "*—Go! Then the Pawnees all leaned forward on their horses and yelled, and away they went. Suddenly, away off to the right, was seen the old dun horse. He did not seem to run. He seemed to sail along like a bird. He passed all the fastest horses, and in a moment he was among the buffalo. First he picked out the spotted calf, and charging up alongside of it, *U-ra-rish!* straight flew the arrow. The calf fell. The boy drew another arrow, and killed a fat cow that was running by. Then he dismounted and began to skin the calf, before any of the other warriors had come up. But when the rider got off the old dun horse, how changed he was! He pranced about and would hardly stand still near the dead buffalo. His back was all right again; his legs were well and fine; and both his eyes were clear and bright.

The boy skinned the calf and the cow that he had killed, and then he packed all the meat on the horse, and put the spotted robe on top of the load, and started back to the camp on foot, leading the dun horse. But even with this heavy load the horse pranced all the time, and was scared at everything he saw. On the way to camp, one of the rich young chiefs of the tribe rode up by the boy and offered him twelve good horses for the spotted robe, so that he could marry the Head Chief's beautiful daughter; but the boy laughed at him and would not sell the robe.

Now, while the boy walked to the camp leading the dun horse, most of the warriors rode back, and one of those that came first to the village went to the old woman and said to her, "Your grandson has killed the spotted calf. " And the old woman said, "Why do you come to tell me this? You ought to be ashamed to make fun of my boy, because he is poor. " The warrior said, "What I have told you is true, " and then he rode away. After a little while another brave rode up to the old woman, and said to her, "Your grandson has killed the spotted calf. " Then the old woman began to cry, she felt so badly because every one made fun of her boy, because he was poor.

Pretty soon the boy came along, leading the horse up to the lodge where he and his grandmother lived. It was a little lodge, just big enough for two, and was made of old pieces of skin that the old woman had picked up, and was tied together with strings of rawhide and sinew. It was the meanest and worst lodge in the village. When the old woman saw her boy leading the dun horse with the load of meat and the robes on it, she was very surprised. The boy said to her, "Here, I have brought you plenty of meat to eat, and here is a robe, that you may have for yourself. Take the meat off the horse. " Then the old woman laughed, for her heart was glad. But when she went to take the meat from the horse's back, he snorted and jumped about, and acted like a wild horse. The old woman looked at him in wonder, and could hardly believe that it was the same horse. So the boy had to take off the meat, for the horse would not let the old woman come near him.

III

That night the horse spoke again to the boy and said, "*Wa-ti-hes Chah'-ra-rat wa-ta*. Tomorrow the Sioux are coming—a large war party. They will attack the village, and you will have a great battle. Now, when the Sioux are all drawn up in line of battle, and are all ready to fight, you jump on to me, and ride as hard as you can, right into the middle of the Sioux, and up to their Head Chief, their greatest warrior, and count *coup* on him, and kill him, and then ride back. Do this four times, and count *coup* on four of the bravest Sioux, and kill them, but don't go again. If you go the fifth time, maybe you will be killed, or else you will lose me. *La-ku'-ta-chix*—remember. " So the boy promised.

The next day it happened as the horse had said, and the Sioux came down and formed in line of battle. Then the boy took his bow and arrows, and jumped on the dun horse, and charged into the midst of them. And when the Sioux saw that he was going to strike their Head Chief, they all shot their arrows at him, and the arrows flew so thickly across each other that they darkened the sky, but none of them hit the boy. And he counted *coup* on the Chief, and killed him, and then rode back. After that he charged again among the Sioux, where they were gathered thickest, and counted *coup* on their bravest warrior, and killed him. And then twice more, until he had gone four times as the horse had told him.

But the Sioux and the Pawnees kept on fighting, and the boy stood around and watched the battle. And at last he said to himself, "I have been four times and have killed four Sioux, and I am all right, I am not hurt anywhere; why may I not go again? " So he jumped on the dun horse, and charged again. But when he got among the Sioux, one Sioux warrior drew an arrow and shot. The arrow struck the dun horse behind the forelegs and pierced him through. And the horse fell down dead. But the boy jumped off, and fought his way through the Sioux, and ran away as fast as he could to the Pawnees. Now, as soon as the horse was killed, the Sioux said to each other: "This horse was like a man. He was brave. He was not like a horse. " And they took their knives and hatchets, and hacked the dun horse and gashed his flesh, and cut him into small pieces.

The Pawnees and Sioux fought all day long, but toward night the Sioux broke and fled.

IV

The boy felt very badly that he had lost his horse; and, after the fight was over, he went out from the village to where it had taken place, to mourn for his horse. He went to the spot where the horse lay, and gathered up all the pieces of flesh, which the Sioux had cut off, and the legs and the hoofs, and put them all together in a pile. Then he went off to the top of a hill near by, and sat down and drew his robe over his head, and began to mourn for his horse.

As he sat there, he heard a great wind-storm coming up, and it passed over him with a loud rushing sound, and after the wind came a rain. The boy looked down from where he sat to the pile of flesh and bones, which was all that was left of his horse, and he could just see it through the rain. And the rain passed by, and his heart was very heavy, and he kept on mourning.

And pretty soon came another rushing wind, and after it a rain; and as he looked through the driving rain toward the spot where the pieces lay, he thought that they seemed to come together and take shape, and that the pile looked like a horse lying down, but he could not see well for the thick rain.

After this came a third storm like the others; and now when he looked toward the horse he thought he saw its tail move from side to side two or three times, and that it lifted its head from the ground. The boy was afraid, and wanted to run away, but he stayed.

And as he waited, there came another storm. And while the rain fell, looking through the rain, the boy saw the horse raise himself up on his forelegs and look about. Then the dun horse stood up.

V

The boy left the place where he had been sitting on the hilltop, and went down to him. When the boy had come near to him, the horse spoke and said: "You have seen how it has been this day; and from this you may know how it will be after this. But *Ti-ra'-wa* has been good, and has let me come back to you. After this, do what I tell you; not any more, not any less. " Then the horse said: "Now lead me off, far away from the camp, behind that big hill, and leave me there to-night, and in the morning come for me; " and the boy did as he was told.

And when he went for the horse in the morning, he found with him a beautiful white gelding, much more handsome than any horse in the tribe. That night the dun horse told the boy to take him again to the place behind the big hill, and to come for him the next morning; and when the boy went for him again, he found with him a beautiful black gelding. And so for ten nights, he left the horse among the hills, and each morning he found a different coloured horse, a bay, a roan, a gray, a blue, a spotted horse, and all of them finer than any horses that the Pawnees had ever had in their tribe before.

Now the boy was rich, and he married the beautiful daughter of the Head Chief, and when he became older he was made Head Chief himself. He had many children by his beautiful wife, and one day when his oldest boy died, he wrapped him in the spotted calf robe and buried him in it. He always took good care of his old grandmother, and kept her in his own lodge until she died. The dun horse was never ridden except at feasts, and when they were going to have a doctors' dance, but he was always led about with the Chief wherever he went. The horse lived in the village for many years, until he became very old. And at last he died.

FOOTNOTES:

[Footnote 7: From "Pawnee Hero Stories and Folk Tales. " Copyright, 1890, by George Bird Grinnell; published by Charles Scribner's Sons.]

XVII

THE GREEDY YOUNGSTER

Once upon a time there were five women who were in a field reaping corn. None of them had any children, but they were all wishing for a child. All at once they found a big goose egg, almost as big as a man's head.

"I saw it first, " said one. "I saw it just as soon as you did, " shouted another. "But I'll have it, " screamed the third, "I saw it first of all. "

Thus they kept on quarrelling and fighting about the egg, and they were very near tearing each other's hair. But at last they agreed that it should belong to them all, and that they should sit on it as the geese do and hatch a gosling. The first woman sat on it for eight days, taking it very comfortably and doing nothing at all, while the others had to work hard both for their own and her living. One of the women began to make some insinuations to her about this.

"Well, I suppose you didn't come out of the egg either before you could chirp, " said the woman who was on the egg, "But I think there is something in this egg, for I fancy I can hear some one inside grumbling every other moment: 'Herring and soup! Porridge and milk! ' You can come and sit for eight days now, and then we will sit and work in turn, all of us. "

So when the fifth in turn had sat for eight days, she heard plainly some one inside the egg screeching for "Herring and soup! Porridge and milk! " And so she made a hole in it; but instead of a gosling out came a baby, but it was awfully ugly, and had a big head and a tiny little body. The first thing it screamed out for, as soon as it put its head outside the egg, was "Herring and soup! Porridge and milk! " And so they called it "the greedy youngster. "

Ugly as he was, they were fond of him at first; but before long he became so greedy that he ate up all the meat they had. When they boiled a dish of soup or a pot of porridge which they thought would be sufficient for all six, he finished it all by himself. So they would not have him any longer.

"I have not had a decent meal since this changeling crept out of the eggshell, " said one of them, and when the youngster heard that they were all of the same opinion, he said he was quite willing to go his way; "if they did not want him, he was sure he did not want them, " and with that he left the place.

After a long time he came to a farm where the fields were full of stones, and he went in and asked for a situation. They wanted a labourer on the farm, and the farmer put him to pick up stones from the field. Yes, the youngster went to work and picked up the stones, some of which were so big that they would make many cartloads; but whether they were big or small, he put them all into his pocket. It did not take him long to finish that job, so he wanted to know what he should do next.

"You will have to get all the stones out of the field, " said the farmer. "I suppose you can't be ready before you have commenced? "

But the youngster emptied his pockets and threw all the stones in a heap. Then the farmer saw that he had finished the work, and he thought he ought to look well after one who was so strong. He must come in and get something to eat, he said. The youngster thought so too, and he alone ate what was prepared both for master and servants, and still he was only half satisfied.

"He is the right sort of man for a labourer, but he is a terrible eater, to be sure, " thought the farmer. "A man like him would eat a poor farmer out of house and home before anybody knew a word about it, " he said. He had no more work for him; it was best for him to go to the king's palace.

The youngster set out for the palace, where he got a place at once. There was plenty of food and plenty of work. He was to be errand boy, and to help the girls to carry wood and water and do other odd jobs. So he asked what he was to do first.

"You had better chop some wood in the mean time, " they said. Yes, he commenced to chop and cut wood till the splinters flew about him. It was not long before he had chopped up everything in the place, both firewood and timber, both rafters and beams, and when he was ready with it, he came in and asked what he was to do now.

"You can finish chopping the wood, " they said.

"There is no more to chop, " he answered.

That could not be possible, thought the overlooker, and had a look into the wood-shed. But yes, the youngster had chopped up everything; he had even cut up the timber and planks in the place. This was vexatious, the overlooker said; and then he told the youngster that he should not taste food until he had gone into the forest and cut just as much timber as he had chopped up for firewood.

The youngster went to the smithy and got the smith to help him to make an axe of five hundredweight of iron, and then he set out for the forest and began to make a regular clearance, not only of the pine and the lofty fir trees, but of everything else which was to be found in the king's forests, and in the neighbours' as well. He did not stop to cut the branches or the tops off, but he left them lying there as if a hurricane had blown them down. He put a proper load on the sledge and put all the horses to it, but they could not even move it; so he took the horses by the heads to give the sledge a start, but he pulled so hard that the horses' heads came off. He then turned the horses out of the shafts and drew the load himself.

When he came to the palace, the king and his overlooker were standing in the hall to give him a scolding for having destroyed the forest—the overlooker had been there and seen what he had been doing. But when the king saw the youngster dragging half the forest after him, he got both angry and afraid; but he thought he had better be a little careful with him, since he was strong.

"Well, you are a wonderful workman, to be sure, " said the king; "but how much do you eat at a time, because I suppose you are hungry now? "

Oh, when he was to have a proper meal of porridge, it would take twelve barrels of meal to make it, thought the youngster; but when he had put that away, he could wait awhile, of course, for his next meal.

It took some time to boil such a dish of porridge, and meantime he was to bring in a little firewood for the cook. He put a lot of wood on a sledge, but when he was coming through the door with it he was a little rough and careless again. The house got almost out of shape, and all the joists creaked; he was very near dragging down the whole palace. When the porridge was nearly ready, they sent him out to call the people home from the fields. He shouted so that the mountains and hills around rang with echoes, but the people did not come quick enough for him. He came to blows with them, and killed twelve of them.

"You have killed twelve men, " said the king; "and you eat for many times twelve; but how many do you work for? "

"For many times twelve as well, " answered the youngster.

When he had finished his porridge, he was to go into the barn to thrash. He took one of the rafters from the roof and made a flail out of it, and when the roof was about to fall in, he took a big pine tree with branches and all and put it up instead of the rafter. So he went on thrashing the grain and the straw and the hay all together. This was doing more damage than good, for the corn and the chaff flew about together, and a cloud of dust arose over the whole palace.

When he had nearly finished thrashing, enemies came into the country, as a war was coming on. So the king told the youngster that he should take men with him to go and meet the enemy and fight them, for the king thought they would surely kill him.

No, he would not have any men with him to be cut to pieces; he would fight by himself, answered the youngster.

"So much the better, " thought the king; "the sooner I shall get rid of him; but he must have a proper club. "

They sent for the smith; he forged a club which weighed a hundredweight. "A very nice thing to crack nuts with, " said the youngster. So the smith made one of three hundredweight. "It would be very well for hammering nails into boots, " was the answer. Well, the smith could not make a bigger one with the men he had. So the youngster set out for the smithy himself, and made a club that weighed five tons, and it took a hundred men to turn it on the anvil. "That one might do for lack of a better, " thought the youngster. He wanted next a bag with some provisions; they had to make one out of fifteen oxhides, and they filled it with food, and away he went down the hill with the bag on his back and the club on his shoulder.

When he came so far that the enemy saw him, they sent a soldier to ask him if he was going to fight them.

"Yes; but wait a little till I have had something to eat, " said the youngster. He threw himself down on the grass and began to eat with the big bag of food in front of him.

But the enemy would not wait, and commenced to fire at him at once, till it rained and hailed around him with bullets.

"I don't mind these crowberries a bit, " said the youngster, and went on eating harder than ever. Neither lead nor iron took any effect upon him, and his bag with food in front of him guarded him against the bullets as if it were a rampart.

So they commenced throwing bomb-shells and firing cannons at him. He only grinned a little every time he felt them.

"They don't hurt me a bit, " he said. But just then he got a bomb-shell right down his windpipe.

"Fy! " he shouted, and spat it out again; but then a chain-shot made its way into his butter-can, and another carried away the piece of food he held between his fingers.

That made him angry; he got up and took his big club and struck the ground with it, asking them if they wanted to take the food out of his mouth, and what they meant by blowing crowberries at him with those pea-shooters of theirs. He then struck the ground again till the hills and rocks rattled and shook, and sent the enemy flying in the air like chaff. This finished the war.

When he came home again, and asked for more work, the king was taken quite aback, for he thought he should have got rid of him in the war. He knew of nothing else but to send him on a message to the devil.

"You had better go to the devil and ask him for my ground-rent, " he said. The youngster took his bag on his back, and started at once. He was not long in getting there, but the devil was gone to court, and there was no one at home but his mother, and she said that she had never heard talk of any ground-rent. He had better call again another time.

"Yes, call again to-morrow is always the cry, " he said; but he was not going to be made a fool of, he told her. He was there, and there he would remain till he got the ground-rent. He had plenty of time to wait. But when he had finished all the food in his bag, the time hung heavy on his hands, and then he asked the old lady for the ground-rent again. She had better pay it now, he said.

"No, she was going to do nothing of the sort, " she said. Her words were as firm as the old fir tree just outside the gates, which was so big that fifteen men could scarcely span it.

But the youngster climbed right up in the top of it and twisted and turned it as if it was a willow, and then he asked her if she was going to pay the ground-rent now.

Yes, she dared not do anything else, and scraped together as much money as he thought he could carry in his bag. He then set out for home with the ground-rent, but as soon as he was gone the devil came home. When he heard that the youngster had gone off with his bag full of money, he first of all gave his mother a hiding, and then he started after him, thinking he would soon overtake him.

He soon came up to him, for he had nothing to carry, and now and then he used his wings; but the youngster had, of course, to keep to the ground with his heavy bag. Just as the devil was at his heels, he began to jump and run as fast as he could. He kept his club behind him to keep the devil off, and thus they went along, the youngster holding the handle and the devil trying to catch hold of the other end of it, till they came to a deep valley. There the youngster made a jump across from the top of one hill to the other, and the devil was in such a hurry to follow him that he ran his head against the club and fell down into the valley and broke his leg, and there he lay.

"There is the ground-rent, " said the youngster when he came to the palace, and threw the bag with the money to the king with such a crash that you could hear it all over the hall.

The king thanked him, and appeared to be well pleased, and promised him good pay and leave of absence if he wished it, but the youngster wanted only more work.

"What shall I do now? " he said.

As soon as the king had had time to consider, he told him that he must go to the hill-troll, who had taken his grandfather's sword. The troll had a castle by the sea, where no one dared to go.

The youngster put some cartloads of food into his bag and set out again. He travelled both long and far, over woods and hills and wild moors, till he came to the big mountains where the troll, who had taken the sword of the king's grandfather, was living.

But the troll seldom came out in the open air, and the mountain was well closed, so the youngster was not man enough to get inside.

So he joined a gang of quarrymen who were living at a farm on top of the hill, and who were quarrying stones in the hills about there. They had never had such help before, for he broke and hammered away at the rocks till the mountain cracked, and big stones of the size of a house rolled down the hill. But when he rested to get his dinner, for which he was going to have one of the cartloads in his bag, he found it was all eaten up.

"I have generally a good appetite myself, " said the youngster; "but the one who has been here can do a trifle more than I, for he has eaten all the bones as well. "

Thus the first day passed; and he fared no better the second. On the third day he set out to break stones again, taking with him the third load of food, but he lay down behind the bag and pretended to be asleep. All of a sudden, a troll with seven heads came out of the mountain and began to eat his food.

"It's all ready for me here, and I will eat, " said the troll.

"We will see about that, " said the youngster, and hit the troll with his club, so the heads rolled down the hill.

So he went into the mountain which the troll had come out of, and in there stood a horse eating out of a barrel of glowing cinders, and behind it stood a barrel of oats.

"Why don't you eat out of the barrel of oats? " asked the youngster.

"Because I cannot turn round, " said the horse.

"But I will soon turn you round, " said the youngster.

"Rather cut my head off, " said the horse.

So he cut its head off, and the horse turned into a fine handsome fellow. He said he had been bewitched, and taken into the mountain and turned into a horse by the troll. He then helped the youngster to find the sword, which the troll had hidden at the bottom of the bed, and in the bed lay the old mother of the troll, asleep and snoring hard.

So they set out for home by water, but when they had got some distance out to sea the old mother came after them. As she could not overtake them, she lay down and began to drink the sea, and she drank till the water fell; but she could not drink the sea dry, and so she burst.

When they came to land, the youngster sent word that the king must come and fetch the sword. He sent four horses, but no, they could not move it; he sent eight, and he sent twelve; but the sword remained where it was. They were not able to stir it from the spot. But the youngster took it and carried it up to the palace alone.

The king could not believe his eyes when he saw the youngster back again. He appeared, however, to be pleased to see him, and promised him land and riches. When the youngster wanted more work, the king said he might set out for an enchanted castle he had, where no one dared to live, and he would have to stop there till he had built a bridge over the sound, so that people could get across to the castle.

If he was able to do this he would reward him handsomely, yes, he would even give him his daughter in marriage, said he.

"Well, I think I can do it, " said the youngster.

No one had ever got away alive; those who had got as far as the castle, lay there killed and torn to pieces as small as barley, and the king thought he should never see him any more if he would go thither.

But the youngster started on his expedition; he took with him the bag of food, a crooked, twisted block of a fir tree, an axe, a wedge, and some chips of the fir root, and the small pauper boy at the palace.

When he came to the sound, he found the river full of ice, and the current ran as strong as in a waterfall; but he stuck his legs to the bottom of the river and waded until he got safe across.

When he had warmed himself and had something to eat, he wanted to go to sleep; but before long he heard such a terrible noise, as if they were turning the castle upside down. The door burst wide open, and he saw nothing but a gaping jaw extending from the threshold up to the lintel.

"There is a mouthful for you, " said the youngster and threw the pauper boy into the swallow: "taste that! But let me see now who you are! Perhaps you are an old acquaintance? "

And so it was; it was the devil who was about again.

They began to play cards, for the devil wanted to try and win back some of the ground-rent which the youngster had got out of his mother by threats, when he was sent by the king to collect it; but the youngster was always the fortunate one, for he put a cross on the back of all the good cards, and when he had won all the money which the devil had upon him, the devil had to pay him out of the gold and silver which was in the castle.

Suddenly the fire went out, so they could not tell the one card from the other.

"We must chop some wood now, " said the youngster, who drove the axe into the fir block, and forced the wedge in; but the twisted, knotty block would not split, although the youngster worked as hard as he could with the axe.

"They say you are strong, " he said to the devil; "just spit on your hands, stick your claws in, and tear away, and let me see what you are made of. "

The devil did so, and put both his fists into the split and pulled as hard as he could, when the youngster suddenly struck the wedge out, and the devil stuck fast in the block and the youngster let him also have a taste of the butt end of his axe on his back. The devil begged and prayed so nicely to be let loose, but the youngster would not listen to anything of the kind unless he promised that he would never come there any more and create any disturbance. He also had to promise that he would build a bridge over the sound, so that people could pass over it at all times of the year, and it should be ready when the ice was gone.

"They are very hard conditions, " said the devil; but there was no other way out of it—if the devil wanted to be set free, he would have to promise it. He bargained, however, that he should have the first soul that went across the bridge. That was to be the toll.

Yes, he should have that, said the youngster. So the devil was let loose, and he started home. But the youngster lay down to sleep, and slept till far into the day.

When the king came to see if he was cut and chopped into small pieces, he had to wade through all the money before he came to his bedside. There was money in heaps and in bags which reached far up the wall, and the youngster lay in bed asleep and snoring hard.

"Lord help me and my daughter, " said the king when he saw that the youngster was alive. Well, all was good and well done, that no one could deny; but there was no hurry talking of the wedding before the bridge was ready.

One day the bridge stood ready, and the devil was there waiting for the toll which he had bargained for.

The youngster wanted the king to go with him and try the bridge, but the king had no mind to do it. So he mounted a horse himself, and put the fat dairy-maid in the palace on the pommel in front of him; she looked almost like a big fir block, and so he rode over the bridge, which thundered under the horse's feet.

"Where is the toll? Where have you got the soul? " cried the devil.

"Why, inside this fir block, " said the youngster; "if you want it you will have to spit in your hands and take it. "

"No, many thanks! If she does not come to me, I am sure I shan't take her, " said the devil. "You got me once into a pinch, and I'll take care you don't get me into another, " and with that he flew straight home to his old mother, and since that time he has never been heard or seen thereabouts.

The youngster went home to the palace and asked for the reward the king had promised him, and when the king wanted to get out of it, and would not stick to what he had promised, the youngster said it was best he got a good bag of food ready for him and he would take his reward himself.

Yes, the king would see to that, and when the bag was ready the youngster asked the king to come outside the door. The youngster then gave the king such a kick, which sent him flying up in the air. The bag he threw after him that he might not be without food; and if he has not come down again by this he is floating about with his bag between heaven and earth to this very day.

XVIII

HANS, WHO MADE THE PRINCESS LAUGH

Once upon a time there was a king, who had a daughter, and she was so lovely that the reports of her beauty went far and wide; but she was so melancholy that she never laughed, and besides she was so grand and proud that she said "No" to all who came to woo her—she would not have any of them, were they ever so fine, whether they were princes or noblemen.

The king was tired of this whim of hers long ago, and thought she ought to get married like other people; there was nothing she need wait for—she was old enough and she would not be any richer either, for she was to have half the kingdom, which she inherited after her mother.

So he made known every Sunday after the service, from the steps outside the church, that he that could make his daughter laugh should have both her and half the kingdom. But if there were any one who tried and could not make her laugh, he would have three red stripes cut out of his back and salt rubbed into them—and, sad to relate, there were many sore backs in that kingdom. Lovers from south and from north, from east and from west, came to try their luck—they thought it was an easy thing to make a princess laugh. They were a queer lot altogether, but for all their cleverness and for all the tricks and pranks they played, the princess was just as serious and immovable as ever.

But close to the palace lived a man who had three sons, and they had also heard that the king had made known that he who could make the princess laugh should have her and half the kingdom.

The eldest of the brothers wanted to try first, and away he went; and when he came to the palace, he told the king he wouldn't mind trying to make the princess laugh.

"Yes, yes! that's all very well, " said the king; "but I am afraid it's of very little use, my man. There have been many here to try their luck, but my daughter is just as sad, and I am afraid it is no good trying. I do not like to see any more suffer on that account. "

84

But the lad thought he would try anyhow. It couldn't be such a difficult thing to make a princess laugh at him, for had not everybody, both grand and simple, laughed so many a time at him when he served as soldier and went through his drill under Sergeant Nils.

So he went out on the terrace outside the princess's windows and began drilling just as if Sergeant Nils himself were there. But all in vain! The princess sat just as serious and immovable as before, and so they took him and cut three broad, red stripes out of his back and sent him home.

He had no sooner arrived home than his second brother wanted to set out and try his luck. He was a schoolmaster, and a funny figure he was altogether. He had one leg shorter than the other, and limped terribly when he walked. One moment he was no bigger than a boy, but the next moment when he raised himself up on his long leg he was as big and tall as a giant—and besides he was great at preaching.

When he came to the palace, and said that he wanted to make the princess laugh, the king thought that it was not so unlikely that he might; "but I pity you, if you don't succeed, " said the king, "for we cut the stripes broader and broader for every one that tries. "

So the schoolmaster went out on the terrace, and took his place outside the princess's window, where he began preaching and chanting imitating seven of the parsons, and reading and singing just like seven of the clerks whom they had had in the parish.

The king laughed at the schoolmaster till he was obliged to hold on to the door-post, and the princess was just on the point of smiling, but suddenly she was as sad and immovable as ever, and so it fared no better with Paul the schoolmaster than with Peter the soldier—for Peter and Paul were their names, you must know!

So they took Paul and cut three red stripes out of his back, put salt into them, and sent him home again.

Well, the youngest brother thought he would have a try next. His name was Hans. But the brothers laughed and made fun of him, and showed him their sore backs. Besides, the father would not give him leave to go, for he said it was no use his trying, who had so little sense; all he could do was to sit in a corner on the hearth, like a cat, rooting about in the ashes and cutting chips. But Hans would not give in—he begged and prayed so long, till they got tired of his whimpering, and so he got leave to go to the king's palace and try his luck.

When he arrived at the palace he did not say he had come to try to make the princess laugh, but asked if he could get a situation there. No, they had no situation for him; but Hans was not so easily put off—they might want one to carry wood and water for the kitchenmaid in such a big place as that, he said. Yes, the king thought so too, and to get rid of the lad he gave him leave to remain there and carry wood and water for the kitchenmaid.

One day, when he was going to fetch water from the brook, he saw a big fish in the water just under an old root of a fir-tree, which the current had carried all the soil away from. He put his bucket quietly under the fish and caught it. As he was going home to the palace, he met an old woman leading a golden goose.

"Good day, grandmother! " said Hans. "That's a fine bird you have got there; and such splendid feathers too! he shines a long way off. If one had such feathers, one needn't be chopping firewood. "

The woman thought just as much of the fish which Hans had in the bucket, and said if Hans would give her the fish he should have the golden goose; and this goose was such that if any one touched it he would be sticking fast to it if he only said: "If you'll come along, then hang on. "

Yes, Hans would willingly exchange on those terms. "A bird is as good as a fish any day, " he said to himself. "If it is as you say, I might use it instead of a fish-hook, " he said to the woman, and felt greatly pleased with the possession of the goose.

He had not gone far before he met another old woman. When she saw the splendid golden goose, she must go and stroke it. She made herself so friendly and spoke so nicely to Hans, and asked him to let her stroke that lovely golden goose of his.

"Oh, yes! " said Hans, "but you mustn't pluck off any of its feathers! "

Just as she stroked the bird, Hans said: "If you'll come along, then hang on! "

The woman pulled and tore, but she had to hang on, whether she would or no, and Hans walked on, as if he only had the goose with him.

When he had gone some distance, he met a man who had a spite against the woman for a trick she had played upon him. When he saw that she fought so hard to get free and seemed to hang on so fast, he thought he might safely venture to pay her off for the grudge he owed her, and so he gave her a kick.

"If you'll come along, then hang on! " said Hans, and the man had to hang on and limp along on one leg, whether he would or no; and when he tried to tear himself loose, he made it still worse for himself, for he was very nearly falling on his back whenever he struggled to get free.

So on they went till they came in the neighborhood of the palace. There they met the king's smith; he was on his way to the smithy, and had a large pair of tongs in his hand. This smith was a merry fellow, and was always full of mad pranks and tricks, and when he saw this procession coming jumping and limping along, he began laughing till he was bent in two, but suddenly he said:

"This must be a new flock of geese for the princess: but who can tell which is goose and which is gander? I suppose it must be the gander toddling on in front. Goosey, goosey! " he called, and pretended to be strewing corn out of his hands as when feeding geese.

But they did not stop. The woman and the man only looked in great rage at the smith for making game of them. So said the smith: "It would be great fun to see if I could stop the whole flock, many as they are! "—He was a strong man, and seized the old man with his tongs from behind in his trousers, and the man shouted and struggled hard, but Hans said:

"If you'll come along, then hang on! "

And so the smith had to hang on too. He bent his back and stuck his heels in the ground when they went up a hill and tried to get away, but it was of no use; he stuck on to the other as if he had been screwed fast in the great vise in the smithy, and whether he liked it or not, he had to dance along with the others.

When they came near the palace, the farm-dog ran against them and barked at them, as if they were a gang of tramps, and when the princess came to look out of her window to see what was the matter, and saw this procession, she burst out laughing. But Hans was not satisfied with that. "Just wait a bit, and she will laugh still louder very soon, " he said, and made a tour round the palace with his followers.

When they came past the kitchen, the door was open and the cook was just boiling porridge, but when she saw Hans and his train after him, she rushed out of the door with the porridge-stick in one hand and a big ladle full of boiling porridge in the other, and she laughed till her sides shook; but when she saw the smith there as well, she thought she would have burst with laughter. When she had had a regular good laugh, she looked at the golden goose again and thought it was so lovely that she must stroke it.

"Hans, Hans! " she cried, and ran after him with the ladle in her hand; "just let me stroke that lovely bird of yours. "

"Rather let her stroke me! " said the smith.

"Very well, " said Hans.

But when the cook heard this, she got very angry. "What is it you say! " she cried, and gave the smith a smack with the ladle.

"If you'll come along, then hang on! " said Hans, and so she stuck fast to the others too, and for all her scolding and all her tearing and pulling, she had to limp along with them.

And when they came past the princess's window again, she was still there waiting for them, but when she saw that they had got hold of the cook too, with the ladle and porridge-stick, she laughed till the king had to hold her up. So Hans got the princess and half the kingdom, and they had a wedding which was heard of far and wide.

XIX

THE STORY OF TOM TIT TOT[8]

Well, once upon a time there were a woman, and she baked five pies. And when they come out of the oven, they was that overbaked the crust were too hard to eat. So she says to her darter:

"Darter, " says she, "put you them there pies on the shelf an' leave 'em there a little, an' they'll come agin—" She meant, you know, the crust 'ud get soft.

But the gal, she says to herself, "Well, if they'll come agin, I'll ate 'em now. " And she set to work and ate 'em all, first and last.

Well, come supper time, the woman she said, "Goo you and git one o' them there pies; I daresay they've come agin, now. "

The gal, she went an' she looked, and there warn't nothin' but the dishes. So back she come and says she, "Noo, they ain't come agin. "

"Not none on 'em? " says the mother.

"Not none on 'em, " says she.

"Well, come agin, or not come agin, " says the woman, "I'll ha' one for supper. "

"But you can't, if they ain't come, " says the gal.

"But I can, " says she. "Goo you and bring the best of 'em. "

"Best or worst, " says the gal, "I've ate 'em all, and you can't ha' one till that's come agin. "

Well, the woman she were wholly bate, and she took her spinnin' to the door to spin, and as she span she sang:

> "My darter ha' ate five, five pies to-day—
> My darter ha' ate five, five pies to-day. "

The king, he were a comin' down the street and he hard her sing, but what she sang he couldn't hare, so he stopped and said:

"What were that you was a singin of, woman? "

The woman, she were ashamed to let him hare what her darter had been a-doin', so she sang, 'stids o' that:

> "My darter ha' spun five, five skeins to-day —
> My darter ha' spun five, five skeins to-day. "

"S'ars o' mine! " said the king, "I never heerd tell of any one as could do that. "

Then he said: "Look you here, I want a wife, and I'll marry your darter. But look you here, " says he, "'leven months out o' the year she shall have all the vittles she likes to eat, and all the gownds she likes to git, and all the cumpny she likes to hev; but the last month o' the year she'll ha' to spin five skeins iv'ry day, an' if she doon't, I shall kill her. "

"All right, " says the woman; for she thowt what a grand marriage that was. And as for them five skeins, when te come tew, there'd be plenty o' ways of gettin' out of it, and likeliest, he'd ha' forgot about it.

Well, so they were married. An' for 'leven months the gal had all the vittles she liked to ate, and all the gownds she liked to git, and all the cumpny she liked to have.

But when the time was gettin' oover, she began to think about them there skeins an' to wonder if he had 'em in mind. But not one word did he say about 'em, an' she whoolly thowt he'd forgot 'em.

Howsivir, the last day o' the last month, he takes her to a room she'd niver set eyes on afore. There worn't nothin' in it but a spinnin' wheel and a stool. An' says he, "Now, me dear, hare you'll be shut in to-morrow with some vittles and some flax, and if you hain't spun five skeins by the night, yar hid'll goo off. "

An' awa' he went about his business.

Well, she were that frightened. She'd allus been such a gatless gal, that she didn't se much as know how to spin, an' what were she to dew to-morrer, with no one to come nigh her to help her? She sat down on a stool in the kitchen, and lork! how she did cry!

Howsivir, all on a sudden she hard a sort of a knockin' low down on the door. She upped and oped it, an' what should she see but a small little black thing with a long tail. That looked up at her right kewrious, an' that said:

"What are yew a-cryin' for? "

"Wha's that to yew? " says she.

"Niver yew mind, " that said, "but tell me what you're a cryin' for. "

"That oon't dew me noo good if I dew, " says she.

"Yew doon't know that, " that said, an' twirled that's tail round.

"Well, " says she, "that oon't dew no harm, if that doon't dew no good, " and she upped and told about the pies an' the skeins an' everything.

"This is what I'll dew, " says the little black thing: "I'll come to yar winder iv'ry mornin' an' take the flax an' bring it spun at night"

"What's your pay? " says she.

That looked out o' the corners o' that's eyes an' that said: "I'll give you three guesses every night to guess my name, an' if you hain't guessed it afore the month's up, yew shall be mine. "

Well, she thowt she'd be sure to guess that's name afore the month was up. "All right, " says she, "I agree. "

"All right, " that says, an' lork! how that twirled that's tail.

Well, the next day, har husband, he took her inter the room, an' there was the flax an' the day's vittles.

"Now, there's the flax, " says he, "an' if that ain't spun up this night, off goo yar hid. " An' then he went out an' locked the door.

He'd hardly goon, when there was a knockin' agin the winder.

She upped and she oped it, and there sure enough was the little oo'd thing a settin' on the ledge.

"Where's the flax? " says he.

"Here te be, " says she. And she gonned it to him.

Well, come the evenin', a knockin' come agin to the winder. She upped an' she oped it, and there were the little oo'd thing, with five skeins of flax on his arm.

"Here te be, " says he, an' he gonned it to her.

"Now, what's my name? " says he.

"What, is that Bill? " says she.

"Noo, that ain't, " says he. An' he twirled his tail.

"Is that Ned? " says she.

"Noo, that ain't, " says he. An' he twirled his tail.

"Well, is that Mark? " says she.

"Noo, that ain't, " says he. An' he twirled his tail harder, an' awa' he flew.

Well, when har husban' he come in, there was the five skeins riddy for him.

"I see I shorn't hev for to kill you to-night, me dare, " says he. "You'll hev yar vittles and yar flax in the mornin', " says he, an' away he goes.

Well, ivery day the flax an' the vittles, they was browt, an' ivery day that there little black impet used for to come mornin's and evenin's. An' all the day the darter, she set a tryin' fur to think of names to say to it when te come at night. But she niver hot on the right one. An' as that got to-warts the ind o' the month, the impet that began for to look soo maliceful, an' that twirled that's tail faster an' faster each time she gave a guess.

At last te came to the last day but one. The impet that come at night along o' the five skeins, an' that said:

"What, hain't yew got my name yet? "

"Is that Nicodemus? " says she.

"Noo, t'ain't, " that says.

"Is that Sammle? " says she.

"Noo, t'ain't, " that says.

"A-well, is that Methusalem? " says she.

"Noo, t'ain't that norther, " he says.

Then that looks at her with that's eyes like a cool o' fire, an that says, "Woman, there's only to-morrer night, an' then yar'll be mine! " An' away te flew.

Well, she felt that horrud. Howsomediver, she hard the king a-comin' along the passage. In he came, an' when he see the five skeins, he says, says he:

"Well, me dare, " says he, "I don't see but what yew'll ha' your skeins ready to-morrer night as well, an' as I reckon I shorn't ha' to kill you, I'll ha' supper in here to-night. " So they brought supper an' another stool for him, and down the tew they sot.

Well, he hadn't eat but a mouthful or so, when he stops and begins to laugh.

"What is it? " says she.

"A-why, " says he, "I was out a-huntin' to-day, an' I got away to a place in the wood I'd never seen afore. An' there was an old chalk pit. An' I heerd a sort of a hummin', kind o'. So I got off my hobby, an' I went right quiet to the pit, an' I looked down. Well, what should there be but the funniest little black thing yew iver set eyes on. An' what was that a dewin' on, but that had a little spinnin' wheel, an' that were a-spinnin' wonnerful fast, an' a-twirlin' that's tail. An' as that span, that sang:

> "Nimmy, nimmy not,
>   My name's Tom Tit Tot. "

Well, when the darter heerd this, she fared as if she could ha' jumped outer her skin for joy, but she di'n't say a word.

Next day, that there little thing looked soo maliceful when he come for the flax. An' when night came, she heerd that a-knockin' agin the winder panes. She oped the winder, an' that come right in on the ledge. That were grinnin' from are to are, an' Oo! tha's tail were twirlin' round so fast.

"What's my name? " that says, as that gonned her the skeins.

"Is that Solomon? " she says, pretendin' to be a-feard.

"Noo, tain't, " that says, an' that come fudder inter the room.

"Well, is that Zebedee? " says she agin.

"Noo, tain't, " says the impet. An' then that laughed an' twirled that's tail till yew cou'n't hardly see it.

"Take time, woman, " that says; "next guess, an' you're mine. " An' that stretched out that's black hands at her.

Well, she backed a step or two, an' she looked at it, and then she laughed out, an' says she, a pointin' of her finger at it:

> "Nimmy, nimmy not,
>   Yar name's Tom Tit Tot. "

Well, when that hard her, that shruck awful an' awa' that flew into the dark, an' she niver saw it noo more.

FOOTNOTES:

[Footnote 8: An old Suffolk tale, given in the dialect of East Anglia.]

XX

THE PEASANT STORY OF NAPOLEON

[Goguelet, an old soldier who fought under Napoleon, tells the story of his wonderful General and Emperor to a group of eager listeners in the country doctor's barn.]

You see, my friends, Napoleon was born in Corsica, a French island, warmed by the sun of Italy, where it is like a furnace, and where the people kill each other, from father to son, all about nothing: that's a way they have. To begin with the marvel of the thing—his mother, who was the handsomest woman of her time, and a knowing one, bethought herself of dedicating him to God, so that he might escape the dangers of his childhood and future life; for she had dreamed that the world was set on fire the day he was born. And, indeed, it was a prophecy! So she asked God to protect him, on condition that Napoleon should restore His holy religion, which was then cast to the ground. Well, that was agreed upon, and we shall see what came of it.

"Follow me closely, and tell me if what you hear is in the nature or man.

"Sure and certain it is that none but a man who conceived the idea of making a compact with God could have passed unhurt through the enemy's lines, through cannon-balls, and discharges of grape-shot that swept the rest of us off like flies, and always respected his head. I had proof of that—I myself—at Eylau. I see him now, as he rode up a height, took his field-glass, looked at the battle, and said, 'All goes well. ' One of those plumed busybodies, who plagued him considerably and followed him everywhere, even to his meals, so they said, thought to play the wag, and took the Emperor's place as he rode away. Ho! in a twinkling, head and plume were off! You must understand that Napoleon had promised to keep the secret of his compact all to himself. That's why all those who followed him, even his nearest friends, fell like nuts—Duroc, Bessières, Lannes—all strong as steel bars, though *he* could bend them as he pleased. Besides—to prove he was the child of God, and made to be the father of soldiers—was he ever known to be lieutenant or captain? No, no; commander-in-chief from the start. He didn't look to be more than twenty-four years of age when he was an old general at the taking of

Toulon, where he first began to show the others that they knew nothing about manoeuvring cannon.

"After that, down came our slip of a general to command the grand army of Italy, which hadn't bread, nor munitions, nor shoes, nor coats—a poor army, as naked as a worm. 'My friends, ' said he, 'here we are together. Get it into your pates that fifteen days from now you will be conquerors—new clothes, good gaiters, famous shoes, and every man with a great-coat; but, my children, to get these things you must march to Milan, where they are. ' And we marched. France, crushed as flat as a bed-bug, straightened up. We were thirty thousand bare-feet against eighty thousand Austrian bullies, all fine men, well set-up. I see 'em now! But Napoleon—he was then only Bonaparte—he knew how to put the courage into us! We marched by night, and we marched by day; we slapped their faces at Montenotte, we thrashed them at Rivoli, Lodi, Arcole, Millesimo, and we never let 'em up. A soldier gets the taste of conquest. So Napoleon whirled round those Austrian generals, who didn't know where to poke themselves to get out of his way, and he pelted 'em well—nipped off ten thousand men at a blow sometimes, by getting round them with fifteen hundred Frenchmen, and then he gleaned as he pleased. He took their cannon, their supplies, their money, their munitions, in short, all they had that was good to take. He fought them and beat them on the mountains, he drove them into the rivers and seas, he bit 'em in the air, he devoured 'em on the ground, and he lashed 'em everywhere. Hey! the grand army feathered itself well; for, d'ye see the Emperor, who was a wit, called up the inhabitants and told them he was there to deliver them. So after that the natives lodged and cherished us; the women too, and very judicious they were. Now here's the end of it. In Ventose, '96—in those times that was the month of March of to-day—we lay cuddled in a corner of Savoie with the marmots; and yet, before that campaign was over, we were masters of Italy, just as Napoleon had predicted; and by the following March—in a single year and two campaigns—he had brought us within sight of Vienna. 'Twas a clean sweep. We devoured their armies, one after the other, and made an end of four Austrian generals. One old fellow, with white hair, was roasted like a rat in the straw at Mantua. Kings begged for mercy on their knees! Peace was won.

"Could a *man* have done that? No; God helped him, to a certainty!

"He divided himself up like the loaves in the Gospel, commanded the battle by day, planned it by night; going and coming, for the sentinels saw him—never eating, never sleeping. So, seeing these prodigies, the soldiers adopted him for their father. Forward, march! Then those others, the rulers in Paris, seeing this, said to themselves: 'Here's a bold one that seems to get his orders from the skies; he's likely to put his paw on France. We must let him loose on Asia; we will send him to America, perhaps that will satisfy him. ' But 't was *written above* for him, as it was for Jesus Christ. The command went forth that he should go to Egypt. See, again, his resemblance to the Son of God. But that's not all. He called together his best veterans, his fire-eaters, the ones he had particularly put the devil into, and he said to them like this: 'My friends, they have given us Egypt to chew up, just to keep us busy, but we'll swallow it whole in a couple of campaigns, as we did Italy. The common soldiers shall be princes and have the land for their own. Forward, march! ' 'Forward, march! ' cried the sergeants, and there we were at Toulon, road to Egypt. At that time the English had all their ships in the sea; but when we embarked, Napoleon said: 'They won't see us. It is just as well that you should know from this time forth that your general has got his star in the sky, which guides and protects us. ' What was said was done. Passing over the sea, we took Malta like an orange, just to quench his thirst for victory; for he was a man who couldn't live and do nothing.

"So here we are in Egypt. Good. Once here, other orders. The Egyptians, d'ye see, are men who, ever since the earth was, have had giants for sovereigns, and armies as numerous as ants; for, you must understand, that's the land of genii and crocodiles, where they've built pyramids as big as our mountains, and buried their kings under them to keep them fresh—an idea that pleased 'em mightily. So then, after we disembarked, the Little Corporal said to us: 'My children, the country you are going to conquer has a lot of gods that you must respect; because Frenchmen ought to be friends with everybody, and fight the nations without vexing the inhabitants. Get it into your skulls that you are not to touch anything at first, for it is all going to be yours soon. Forward, march! ' So far, so good. But all those people of Africa, to whom Napoleon was foretold under the name of Kébir-Bonaberdis—a word of their lingo that means 'the sultan fires'—were afraid as the devil of him. So the Grand Turk, and Asia, and Africa had recourse to magic. They sent us a demon, named the Mahdi, supposed to have descended from heaven on a white horse, which, like its master, was bullet-proof; and both of them lived on air, without food to support them. There are some that say they saw them; but I can't give you any reasons to make you certain about that. The rulers of Arabia and the Mamelukes tried to make their troopers believe that the Mahdi could keep them from perishing in battle; and they pretended he was an angel sent from heaven to fight Napoleon and get back Solomon's seal. Solomon's seal was part of their paraphernalia which they vowed our general had stolen. You must understand that we'd given 'em a good many wry faces, in spite of what he had said to us.

"Now, tell me how they knew that Napoleon had a pact with God? Was that natural, d'ye think?

"They held to it in their minds that Napoleon commanded the genii, and could pass hither and thither in the twinkling of an eye, like a bird. The fact is, he was everywhere. At last, it came to his carrying off a queen beautiful as the dawn, for whom he had offered all his treasure, and diamonds as big as pigeon's eggs—a bargain which the Mameluke to whom she particularly belonged positively refused, although he had several others. Such matters when they come to that pass, can't be settled without a great many battles; and, indeed, there was no scarcity of battles; there was fighting enough to please everybody. We were in line at Alexandria, at Gizeh, and before the Pyramids; we marched in the sun and through the sand, where some, who had the dazzles, saw water that they couldn't drink, and shade where their flesh was roasted. But we made short work of the Mamelukes; and everybody else yielded at the voice of Napoleon, who took possession of Upper and Lower Egypt, Arabia, and even the capitals of kingdoms that were no more, where there were thousands of statues and all the plagues of Egypt, more particularly lizards—a mammoth of a country where everybody could take his acres of land for as little as he pleased. Well, while Napoleon was busy with his affairs inland—where he had it in his head to do fine things—the English burned his fleet at Aboukir; for they were always looking about them to annoy us. But Napoleon, who had the respect of the East and of the West, whom the Pope called his son, and the cousin of Mohammed called 'his dear father, ' resolved to punish England, and get hold of India in exchange for his fleet. He was just about to take us across the Red Sea into Asia, a country where there are diamonds and gold to pay the soldiers and palaces for bivouacs, when the Mahdi made a treaty with the plague, and sent it down to hinder our victories. Halt! The army to a man defiled at that parade; and few they were who came back on their feet.

Dying soldiers couldn't take Saint-Jean d'Acre, though they rushed at it three times with generous and martial obstinacy. The Plague was the strongest. No saying to that enemy, 'My good friend. ' Every soldier lay ill. Napoleon alone was fresh as a rose, and the whole army saw him drinking in pestilence without its doing him a bit of harm.

"Ha! my friends! will you tell me that *that's* in the nature of a mere man?

"The Mamelukes, knowing we were all in the ambulances, thought they could stop the way; but that sort of joke wouldn't do with Napoleon. So he said to his demons, his veterans, those that had the toughest hide, 'Go, clear me the way. ' Junot, a sabre of the first cut, and his particular friend, took a thousand men, no more, and ripped up the army of the pacha who had had the presumption to put himself in the way. After that, we came back to headquarters at Cairo. Now, here's another side of the story. Napoleon absent, France was letting herself be ruined by the rulers in Paris, who kept back the pay of the soldiers of the other armies, and their clothing, and their rations; left them to die of hunger, and expected them to lay down the law to the universe without taking any trouble to help them. Idiots! who amused themselves by chattering, instead of putting their own hands in the dough. Well, that's how it happened that our armies were beaten, and the frontiers of France were encroached upon: THE MAN was nor there. Now observe, I say *man* because that's what they called him; but 'twas nonsense, for he had a star and all its belongings; it was we who were only men. He taught history to France after his famous battle of Aboukir, where, without losing more than three hundred men, and with a single division, he vanquished the grand army of the Turk, seventy-five thousand strong, and hustled more than half of it into the sea, r-r-rah!

"That was his last thunder-clap in Egypt. He said to himself, seeing the way things were going in Paris, 'I am the saviour of France; I know it, and I must go. ' But, understand me, the army didn't know he was going, or they'd have kept him by force and made him Emperor of the East. So now we were sad; for He was gone who was all our joy. He left the command to Kléber, a big mastiff, who came off duty at Cairo, assassinated by an Egyptian, whom they put to death by empaling him on a bayonet; that's the way they guillotine people down there. But it makes 'em suffer so much that a soldier had pity on the criminal and gave him his canteen; and then, as soon as the Egyptian had drunk his fill, he gave up the ghost with all the pleasure in life. But that's a trifle we couldn't laugh at then. Napoleon embarked in a cockleshell, a little skiff that was nothing at all, though 'twas called 'Fortune; ' and in a twinkling, under the nose of England, who was blockading him with ships of the line, frigates, and anything that could hoist a sail, he crossed over, and there he was in France. For he always had the power, mind you, of crossing the seas at one straddle.

"Was that a human man? Bah!

"So, one minute he is at Fréjus, the next in Paris. There, they all adore him; but he summons the government. 'What have you done with my children, the soldiers? ' he says to the lawyers. 'You're a mob of rascally scribblers; you are making France a mess of pottage, and snapping your fingers at what people think of you. It won't do; and I speak the opinion of everybody. ' So, on that, they wanted to battle with him and kill him—click! he had 'em locked up in barracks, or flying out of windows, or drafted among his followers, where they were as mute as fishes and as pliable as a quid of tobacco. After that stroke—consul! And then, as it was not for him to doubt the Supreme Being, he fulfilled his promise to the good God, who, you see, had kept His word to him. He gave Him back His churches, and reestablished His religion; the bells rang for God and for him: and lo! everybody was pleased; *primo*, the priests, whom he saved from being harassed; *secundo*, the bourgeois, who thought only of their trade, and no longer had to fear the *rapiamus* of the law, which had got to be unjust; *tertio*, the nobles, for he forbade they should be killed, as, unfortunately, the people had got the habit of doing.

"But he still had the Enemy to wipe out; and he wasn't the man to go to sleep at a mess-table, because, d'ye see, his eye looked over the whole earth as if it were no bigger than a man's head. So then he appeared in Italy, like as though he had stuck his head through the window. One glance was enough. The Austrians were swallowed up at Marengo like so many gudgeons by a whale! Ouf! The French eagles sang their pæans so loud that all the world heard them—and it sufficed! 'We won't play that game any more, ' said the German. 'Enough, enough! ' said all the rest. To sum up: Europe backed down, England knocked under. General peace; and the kings and the peoples made believe kiss each other. That's the time when the Emperor invented the Legion of Honour—and a fine thing, too. 'In France'—this is what he said at Boulogne before the whole army—

'every man is brave. So the citizen who does a fine action shall be sister to the soldier, and the soldier shall be his brother, and the two shall be one under the flag of honour. '

"We, who were down in Egypt, now came home. All was changed! He left us general, and hey! in a twinkling we found him EMPEROR. France gave herself to him, like a fine girl to a lancer. When it was done—to the satisfaction of all, as you may say—a sacred ceremony took place, the like of which was never seen under the canopy of the skies. The Pope and the cardinals, in their red and gold vestments, crossed the Alps expressly to crown him before the army and the people, who clapped their hands. There is one thing that I should do very wrong not to tell you. In Egypt, in the desert close to Syria, the RED MAN came to him on the Mount of Moses, and said, 'All is well. ' Then, at Marengo, the night before the victory, the same Red Man appeared before him for the second time, standing erect and saying: 'Thou shalt see the world at thy feet; thou shalt be Emperor of France, King of Italy, master of Holland, sovereign of Spain, Portugal, and the Illyrian provinces, protector of Germany, saviour of Poland, first eagle of the Legion of Honour—all. ' This Red Man, you understand, was his genius, his spirit—a sort of satellite who served him, as some say, to communicate with his star. I never really believed that. But the Red Man himself is a true fact. Napoleon spoke of him, and said he came to him in troubled moments, and lived in the palace of the Tuileries under the roof. So, on the day of the coronation, Napoleon saw him for the third time; and they were in consultation over many things.

"After that, Napoleon went to Milan to be crowned king of Italy, and there the grand triumph of the soldier began. Every man who could write was made an officer. Down came pensions; it rained duchies; treasures poured in for the staff which didn't cost France a penny; and the Legion of Honour provided incomes for the private soldiers—of which I receive mine to this day. So here were the armies maintained as never before on this earth. But besides that, the Emperor, knowing that he was to be the emperor of the whole world, bethought him of the bourgeois, and to please them he built fairy monuments, after their own ideas, in places where you'd never think to find any. For instance, suppose you were coming back from Spain and going to Berlin—well, you'd find triumphal arches along the way, with common soldiers sculptured on the stone, every bit the same as generals. In two or three years, and without imposing taxes on any of you, Napoleon filled his vaults with gold, built palaces, made bridges, roads, scholars, fêtes, laws, vessels, harbours, and spent millions upon millions—such enormous sums that he could, so they tell me, have paved France from end to end with five-franc pieces, if he had had a mind to.

"Now, when he sat at ease on his throne, and was master of all, so that Europe waited his permission to do his bidding, he remembered his four brothers and his three sisters, and he said to us, as it might be in conversation, in an order of the day, 'My children, is it right that the blood relations of your Emperor should be begging their bread? No. I wish to see them in splendour like myself. It becomes, therefore, absolutely necessary to conquer a kingdom for each of them—to the end that Frenchmen may be masters over all lands, that the soldiers of the Guard shall make the whole earth tremble, that France may spit where she likes, and that all the nations shall say to her, as it is written on my copper coins, '*God protects you!* ' 'Agreed! ' cried the army. 'We'll go fish for thy kingdoms with our bayonets. ' Ha! there was no backing down, don't you see! If he had taken it into his head to conquer the moon, we should have made ready, packed knapsacks, and clambered up; happily, he didn't think of it. The kings of the countries, who liked their comfortable thrones, were, naturally, loath to budge, and had to have their ears pulled; so then—Forward, march! We did march; we got there; and the earth once more trembled to its centre. Hey! the men and the shoes he used up in those days! The enemy dealt us such blows that none but the grand army could have borne the fatigue of it. But you are not ignorant that a Frenchman is born a philosopher, and knows that a little sooner, or a little later, he has got to die. So we were ready to die without a word, for we liked to see the Emperor doing *that* on the geographies. "

Here the narrator nimbly described a circle with his foot on the floor of the barn.

"And Napoleon said, 'There, that's to be a kingdom. ' And a kingdom it was. Ha! the good times! The colonels were generals; the generals, marshals; and the marshals, kings. There's one of 'em still on his throne, to prove it to Europe; but he's a Gascon and a traitor to France for keeping that crown; and he doesn't blush for shame as he ought to do, because crowns, don't you see, are made of gold. I who am speaking to you, I have seen, in Paris, eleven kings and a mob of princes surrounding Napoleon like the rays of the sun. You understand, of course, that every soldier had the chance to mount a throne, provided always he had the merit; so a corporal of the Guard was a sight to be looked at as he walked along, for each man had his share in the victory, and 'twas plainly set forth in the bulletin. What victories they were! Austerlitz, where the army manoeuvred as if on parade; Eylau, where we drowned the Russians in a lake, as though Napoleon had blown them into it with the breath of his mouth; Wagram, where the army fought for three days without grumbling. We won as many battles as there are saints in the calendar. It was proved then, beyond a doubt, that Napoleon had the sword of God in his scabbard. The soldiers were his friends; he made them his children; he looked after us, he saw that we had shoes, and shirts, and great-coats, and bread, and cartridges; but he always kept up his majesty; for, don't you see, 'twas his business to reign. No matter for that, however; a sergeant, and even a common soldier, could say to him, 'my Emperor, ' just as you say to me sometimes, 'my good friend. ' He gave us an answer if we appealed to him; he slept in the snow like the rest of us; and, indeed, he had almost the air of a human man. I who speak to you, I have seen him with his feet among the grape-shot, and no more uneasy than you are now— standing steady, looking through his field-glass, and minding his business. 'Twas that kept the rest of us quiet. I don't know how he did it, but when he spoke he made our hearts burn within us; and to show him we were his children, incapable of balking, didn't we rush at the mouths of the rascally cannon, that belched and vomited shot and shell, without so much as saying, 'Look out! ' Why! the dying must needs raise their heads to salute him and cry, 'LONG LIVE THE EMPEROR! '

"I ask you, was that natural? would they have done that for a human man?

"Well, after he had settled the world, the Empress Josephine, his wife, a good woman all the same, managed matters so that she did not bear him any children, and he was obliged to give her up, though he loved her considerably. But, you see, he had to have little ones for reasons of state. Hearing of this, all the sovereigns of Europe quarrelled as to which of them should give him a wife. And he married, so they told us, an Austrian archduchess, daughter of Cæsar, an ancient man about whom people talk a good deal, and not in France only—where any one will tell you what he did—but in Europe. It is all true, for I myself who address you at this moment, I have been on the Danube, and have seen the remains of a bridge built by that man, who, it seems, was a relation of Napoleon in

Rome, and that's how the Emperor got the inheritance of that city for his son. So after the marriage, which was a fête for the whole world, and in honour of which he released the people of ten years' taxes— which they had to pay all the same, however, because the assessors didn't take account of what he said—his wife had a little one, who was King of Rome. Now, there's a thing that had never been seen on this earth; never before was a child born a king with his father living. On that day a balloon went up in Paris to tell the news to Rome, and that balloon made the journey in one day.

"Now, is there any man among you who will stand up here and declare to me that all that was human? No; it was *written above*; and may the scurvy seize 'em who deny that he was sent by God himself for the triumph of France!

"Well, here's the Emperor of Russia, that used to be his friend, he gets angry because Napoleon didn't marry a Russian; so he joins with the English, our enemies—to whom our Emperor always wanted to say a couple of words in their burrows, only he was prevented. Napoleon gets angry too; an end had to be put to such doings; so he says to us: 'Soldiers! you have been masters of every capital in Europe, except Moscow, which is now the ally of England. To conquer England, and India which belongs to the English, it becomes our peremptory duty to go to Moscow, ' Then he assembled the greatest army that ever trailed its gaiters over the globe; and so marvellously in hand it was that he reviewed a million of men in one day. 'Hourra! '[9] cried the Russians. Down came all Russia and those animals of Cossacks in a flock. 'Twas nation against nation, a general hurly-burly, and beware who could; 'Asia against Europe, ' as the Red Man had foretold to Napoleon. 'Enough, ' cried the Emperor, 'I'll be ready. '

"So now, sure enough, came all the kings, as the Red Man had said, to lick Napoleon's hand! Austria, Prussia, Bavaria, Saxony, Poland, Italy, every one of them were with us, flattering us; ah, it was fine! The eagles never cawed so loud as at those parades, perched high above the banners of all Europe. The Poles were bursting with joy, because Napoleon was going to release them; and that's why France and Poland are brothers to this day. 'Russia is ours, ' cried the army. We plunged into it well-supplied; we marched and we marched—no Russians. At last we found the brutes entrenched on the banks of the Moskva. That's where I won my cross, and I've got the right to say it was a damnable battle. This was how it came about. The Emperor was anxious. He had seen the Red Man, who said to him 'My son, you are going too fast for your feet; you will lack men; friends will betray you. ' So the Emperor offered peace. But before signing, 'Let us drub those Russians! ' he said to us. 'Done! ' cried the army. 'Forward, march! ' said the sergeants. My clothes were in rags, my shoes worn out, from trudging along those roads, which are very uncomfortable ones; but no matter! I said to myself, 'As it's the last of our earthquakings, I'll go into it, tooth and nail! ' We were drawn up in line before the great ravine—front seats, as 'twere. Signal given; and seven hundred pieces of artillery began a conversation that would bring the blood from your ears. Then—must do justice to one's enemies—the Russians let themselves be killed like Frenchmen; they wouldn't give way; we couldn't advance. 'Forward! ' some one cried, 'here comes the Emperor! ' True enough; he passed at a gallop, waving his hand to let us know we must take the redoubt. He inspired us; on we ran; I was the first in the ravine. Ha! my God! how the lieutenants fell, and the colonels, and the soldiers! No matter! all the more shoes for those that had none, and epaulets for the clever ones who knew how to read. 'Victory! ' cried the whole line; 'Victory! '—and, would you believe it? a thing never seen before, there lay twenty-five thousand Frenchmen on the ground. 'Twas like mowing down a wheat-field; only in place of the ears of wheat put the heads of men! We were sobered by this time—those who were left alive. The MAN rode up; we made the circle round him. Ha! he knew how to cajole his children; he could be amiable when he liked, and feed 'em with words when their stomachs were ravenous with the hunger of wolves. Flatterer! he distributed the crosses himself, he uncovered to the dead, and then he cried to us, 'On! to Moscow! ' 'To Moscow! ' answered the army.

"We took Moscow. Would you believe it? the Russians burned their own city! 'Twas a haystack six miles square, and it blazed for two days. The buildings crashed like slates, and showers of melted iron and lead rained down upon us, which was naturally horrible. I may say to you plainly, it was like a flash of lightning on our disasters. The Emperor said, 'We have done enough; my soldiers shall rest here. ' So we rested awhile, just to get the breath into our bodies and the flesh on our bones, for we were really tired. We took possession of the golden cross that was on the Kremlin; and every soldier brought away with him a small fortune. But out there the winter sets in a month earlier—a thing those fools of science didn't properly explain. So, coming back, the cold nipped us. No longer an army — do you hear me? —no longer any generals, no longer any sergeants even. 'Twas the reign of wretchedness and hunger—a reign of equality at last. No one thought of anything but to see France once more; no one stooped to pick up his gun or his money if he dropped them; each man followed his nose, and went as he pleased without caring for glory. The weather was so bad the Emperor couldn't see his star; there was something between him and the skies. Poor man! it made him ill to see his eagles flying away from victory. Ah! 'twas a mortal blow, you may believe me.

"Well, we got to the Beresina, My friends, I can affirm to you by all that is most sacred, by my honour, that since mankind came into the world, never, never was there seen such a fricassee of any army— guns, carriages, artillery-waggons—in the midst of such snows, under such relentless skies! The muzzles of the muskets burned our hands if we touched them, the iron was so cold. It was there that the army was saved by the pontoniers, who were firm at their post; and there that Gondrin—sole survivor of the men who were bold enough to go into the water and build the bridges by which the army crossed—that Gondrin, here present, admirably conducted himself, and saved us from the Russians, who, I must tell you, still respected the grand army, remembering its victories. And, " he added, pointing to Gondrin, who was gazing at him with the peculiar attention of a deaf man, "Gondrin is a finished soldier, a soldier who is honour itself, and he merits your highest esteem.

"I saw the Emperor, " he resumed, "standing by the bridge, motionless, not feeling the cold—was that human? He looked at the destruction of his treasure, his friends, his old Egyptians. Bah! all that passed him, women, army-waggons, artillery, all were shattered, destroyed, ruined. The bravest carried the eagles; for the eagles, d'ye see, were France, the nation, all of you! they were the civil and the military honour that must be kept pure; could their heads be lowered because of the cold? It was only near the Emperor that we warmed ourselves, because when he was in danger we ran, frozen as we were—we, who wouldn't have stretched a hand to save a friend. They told us he wept at night over his poor family of soldiers. Ah! none but he and Frenchmen could have got themselves out of that business. We did get out, but with losses, great losses, as I tell you. The Allies captured our provisions. Men began to betray him, as the Red Man predicted. Those chatterers in Paris, who had held their tongues after the Imperial Guard was formed, now thought he was dead; so they hoodwinked the prefect of police, and hatched a conspiracy to overthrow the empire. He heard of it; it worried him. He left us, saying: 'Adieu, my children; guard the outposts; I shall return to you, ' Bah! without him nothing went right; the generals lost their heads, the marshals talked nonsense and committed follies; but that was not surprising, for Napoleon, who was kind, had fed 'em on gold; they had got as fat as lard, and wouldn't stir; some stayed in camp when they ought to have been warming the backs of the enemy who was between us and France.

"But the Emperor came back, and he brought recruits, famous recruits; he changed their backbone and made 'em dogs of war, fit to set their teeth into anything; and he brought a guard of honour, a fine body indeed! —all bourgeois, who melted away like butter on a gridiron.

"Well, spite of our stern bearing, here's everything going against us; and yet the army did prodigies of valour. Then came battles on the mountains, nations against nations—Dresden, Lützen, Bautzen. Remember these days, all of you, for 'twas then that Frenchmen were so particularly heroic that a good grenadier only lasted six months. We triumphed always; yet there were those English, in our rear, rousing revolts against us with their lies! No matter, we cut our way home through the whole pack of the nations. Wherever the Emperor showed himself we followed him; for if, by sea or land, he gave us the word 'Go! ' we went. At last, we were in France; and many a poor foot-soldier felt the air of his own country restore his soul to satisfaction, spite of the wintry weather. I can say for myself that it refreshed my life. Well, next, our business was to defend France, our country, our beautiful France, against, all Europe, which resented our having laid down the law to the Russians, and pushed them back into their dens so that they couldn't eat us up alive, as northern nations, who are dainty and like southern flesh, have a habit of doing—at least, so I've heard some generals say. Then the Emperor saw his own father-in-law, his friends whom he had made kings, and the scoundrels to whom he had given back their thrones, all against him. Even Frenchmen, and allies in our own ranks, turned against us under secret orders, as at the battle of Leipsic. Would common soldiers have been capable of such wickedness? Three times a day men were false to their word—and they called themselves princes!

"So, then, France was invaded. Wherever the Emperor showed his lion face, the enemy retreated; and he did more prodigies in defending France than ever he had done in conquering Italy, the

East, Spain, Europe, and Russia. He meant to bury every invader under the sod, and teach 'em to respect the soil of France. So he let them get to Paris, that he might swallow them at a mouthful, and rise to the height of his genius in a battle greater than all the rest—a mother-battle, as 'twere. But there, there! the Parisians were afraid for their twopenny skins, and their trumpery shops; they opened the gates. Then the Ragusades began, and happiness ended. The Empress was fooled, and the white banner flaunted from the windows. The generals whom he had made his nearest friends abandoned him for the Bourbons—a set of people no one had heard tell of. The Emperor bade us farewell at Fontainebleau: 'Soldiers! '—I can hear him now; we wept like children; the flags and the eagles were lowered as if for a funeral: it was, I may well say it to you, it was the funeral of the Empire; her dapper armies were nothing now but skeletons. So he said to us, standing there on the portico of his palace: 'My soldiers! we are vanquished by treachery; but we shall meet in heaven, the country of the brave. Defend my child, whom I commit to you. Long live Napoleon II! ' He meant to die, that no man should look upon Napoleon vanquished; he took poison, enough to have killed a regiment, because, like Jesus Christ before his Passion, he thought himself abandoned of God and his talisman. But the poison did not hurt him.

"See again! he found he was immortal.

"Sure of himself, knowing he must ever be THE EMPEROR, he went for a while to an island to study out the nature of these others, who, you may be sure, committed follies without end. Whilst he bided his time down there, the Chinese, and the wild men on the coast of Africa, and the Barbary States, and others who are not at all accommodating, know so well he was more than man that they respected his tent, saying to touch it would be to offend God. Thus, d'ye see, when these others turned him from the doors of his own France, he still reigned over the whole world. Before long he embarked in the same little cockleshell of a boat he had had in Egypt, sailed round the beard of the English, set foot in France, and France acclaimed him. The sacred cuckoo flew from spire to spire; all France cried out with one voice, 'LONG LIVE THE EMPEROR! ' In this region, here, the enthusiasm for that wonder of the ages was, I may say, solid. Dauphine behaved well; and I am particularly pleased to know that her people wept when they saw, once more, the gray top-coat. March first it was, when Napoleon landed with two hundred men to conquer that kingdom of France and of Navarre, which, on the twentieth of the same month was again the French Empire. On that day our MAN was in Paris; he had made a clean sweep, recovered his dear France, and gathered his veterans together by saying no more than three words, 'I am here. '

"'Twas the greatest miracle God had yet done! Before *him*, did ever man recover an empire by showing his hat? And these others, who thought they had subdued France! Not they! At sight of the eagles, a national army sprang up, and we marched to Waterloo. There, the Guard died at one blow. Napoleon, in despair, threw himself three times before the cannon of the enemy without obtaining death. We saw that. The battle was lost. That night the Emperor called his old soldiers to him; on the field soaked with our blood he burned his banners and his eagles—his poor eagles, ever victorious, who cried 'Forward' in the battles, and had flown the length and breadth of Europe, *they* were saved the infamy of belonging to the enemy: all the treasures of England couldn't get her a tail-feather of them. No more eagles—the rest is well known. The Red Man went over to the Bourbons, like the scoundrel that he is. France is crushed; the soldier is nothing; they deprive him of his dues; they discharge him to make room for broken-down nobles—ah, 'tis pitiable! They seized Napoleon by treachery; the English nailed him on a desert island in mid-ocean on a rock raised ten thousand feet above the earth; and there he is, and will be, till the Red Man gives him back his power for the happiness of France. These others say he's dead. Ha, dead! 'Tis easy to see they don't know Him. They tell that fib to catch the people, and feel safe in their hovel of a government. Listen! the truth at the bottom of it all is that his friends have left him alone on the desert isle to fulfil a prophecy, for I forgot to say that his name, Napoleon, means 'lion of the desert. ' Now this that I tell you is true as the Gospel. All other tales that you hear about the Emperor are follies without common-sense; because, d'ye see, God never gave to child of woman born the right to stamp his name in red as *he* did, on the earth, which forever shall remember him! Long live Napoleon, the father of his people and of the soldier! "

THE END

FOOTNOTES:

[Footnote 9: Battle-cry of the Cossacks.]

Lightning Source UK Ltd.
Milton Keynes UK
UKHW010634140622
404409UK00001B/95